Watch me Follow

Watch Me Follow

Cover Design:
Talia's Book Covers

Editing:
Ace Gray

Interior Design & Formatting:
Christine Borgford, Type A Formatting

HARLOE RAE

playlist

Wild Horses by The Rolling Stones

H.O.L.Y. by Florida Georgia Line

Creepin' by Eric Church

Greatest Love Story by DJ Kyotee

Every Little Thing by Carly Pearce

Blame It on Me by George Ezra

Fix You by Coldplay

The Night We Met by Lord Huron

Too Much to Ask by Niall Horan

Dream Big by Ryan Shupe & The Rubberband

In the Name of Love by Martin Garrix

Your Song by Rita Ora

Rise Up by Andra Day

You Are My Sunshine by Jasmine Thompson

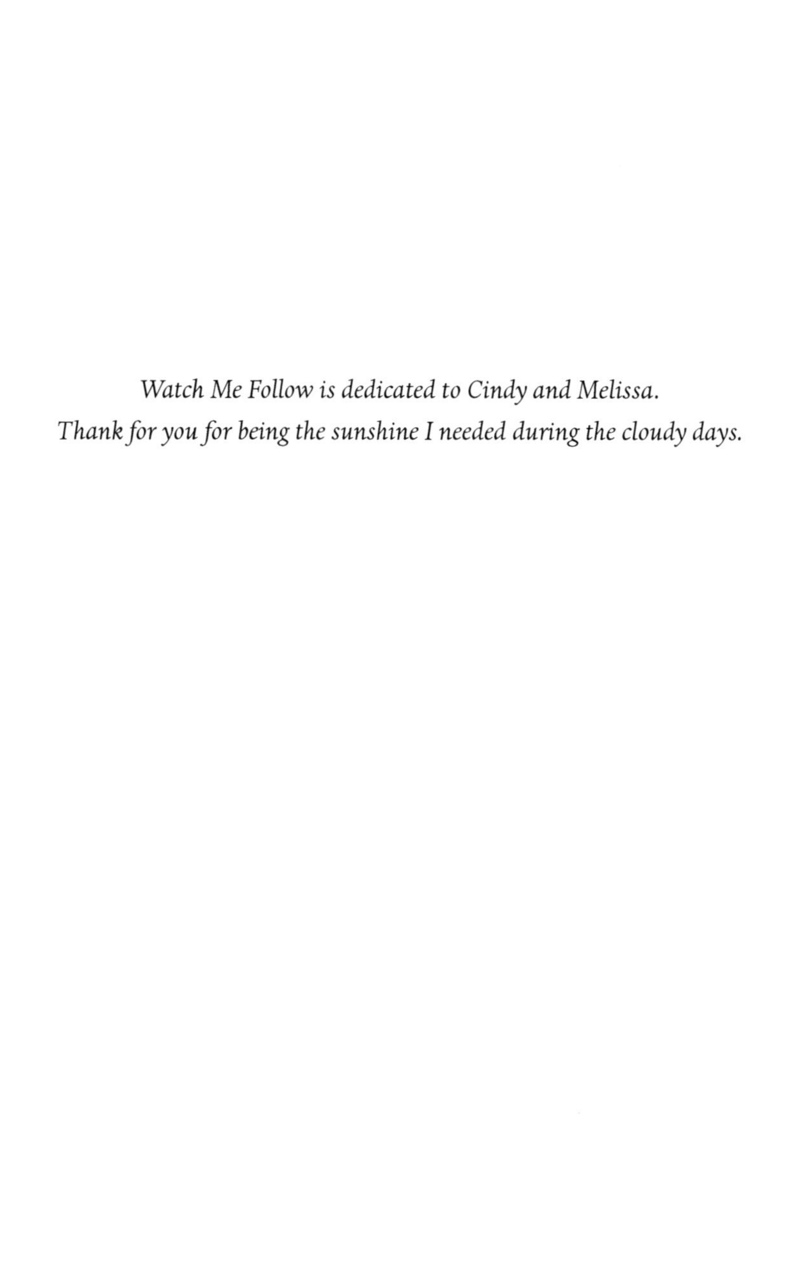

Watch Me Follow is dedicated to Cindy and Melissa.
Thank for you for being the sunshine I needed during the cloudy days.

about

WATCH me FOLLOW

Creep. Freak. Crazy Eyes.

I've heard it all.

Over the years, they've slammed me with every demeaning name in the book.

Their taunts warped me like a steady stream of poison.

Anger replaced anxiety as I started believing the cruelty spat my way.

Until she showed up and changed everything.

Lennon Bennett is pure innocence—warm sunshine breaking apart my stormy existence.

She's everything good and maybe I can be too.

For her. With her. Because of her.

Lennon doesn't know I'm beckoned closer with each breath.

She isn't aware that I'm completely consumed with her.

It's become my sole purpose to protect her, by any means necessary.

But if she discovers the depth of my obsession, it will be the end of me.

So, I remain in the shadows.

Waiting. Watching. Wanting.

She'll be my first. My last. My only.

prologue
RYKER

For the first time in my life, I don't feel alone. This blinding ray of sunshine has suddenly appeared in the form of a beautiful girl.

SHE'S SMILING AT ME.

Lennon Bennett is the most beautiful creature to ever grace this fucked up planet and she's currently turned around in her seat, grinning at me.

That's never happened before so I'm not sure how to react. I fight the initial urge to shield my face with the thick curtain of hair tucked behind my ear because I want her to see me. Shock streaks through me like lightning as her unwavering stare stays fixed on me—the boy everyone always looks away from. I'm not prepared to handle this sort of blatant attention, especially from her. My heart threatens to burst as I'm consumed by her gaze but my face remains blank, like usual.

"Hi," Lennon barely whispers. "Can I, um, borrow a pencil?"

Her sugary voice is soft but clear, sinking deep into my bones. Sweat dots my brow as I blindly reach into my backpack, refusing to break eye contact. My clumsy fingers fumble a few times before getting a grip on one and hold it out to her.

"Oh, uh . . . thanks," she mumbles as red colors her cheeks.

Why is she blushing?

Confusion clogs any attempt at processing this interaction while I scan her flushed face. My head jerks in acknowledgement but my lips remain frozen in a flat line.

Lennon clears her throat before asking, "Can I have a piece of paper too?"

I carelessly tear a sheet from my notebook and offer it without hesitation. Her shoulders shake with a soundless giggle as she thanks me and takes the paper from my trembling grasp. Lennon doesn't look away and I wonder what she sees as she keeps staring at me. After a moment of shared silence, she sighs heavily and the smile slips from her lips.

Before I can consider Lennon's reaction further or try forcing a response, she twists back around and effectively breaks our connection.

I fucking blew it.

She talked to me and I said nothing, which is exactly what I am—fucking nothing. Why do I even bother? Maybe because the small slice of hope surviving in my starved heart believes she could be different.

Ever since Lennon started school here a few weeks ago, my thoughts have rarely strayed from her. Each glorious piece of her fuels my fantasies and drags me deeper into obsession. I'm totally infatuated with her, but what the hell am I supposed to do about it?

Keep staring like a creep.

Lennon's skin glows with a bronze tan even though it's still spring in Michigan. I'm not sure where she moved from but it must have been warm. She's very short, tiny really, which makes protective instincts I didn't know existed rattle inside me. Even though I never touch anyone, my arms ache with the urge to wrap around her skinny waist and pull her close. Lennon's glossy dark hair appears to be made of the softest silk. The long waves shimmer whenever she shifts her head and constantly lures me into a trance. Her sparkling aqua eyes remind me of a tropical sea. Today is the first time her smile has been cast my way and the beaming sight is by far my favorite. Possessiveness has been slowly spreading through me but I'll never be able to let her go now that she's acknowledged me. The realization hits hard and knocks any remaining sense loose.

Not that I had much to begin with—at least according to everyone else.

I slouch deeper into my desk as the dark memories wash over me. Every nasty name in the book has been spat my way, but I stopped listening years ago. The verbal assaults all sound the same eventually, whether coming from my worthless parents or the jerkoffs currently surrounding me. The constant onslaught makes keeping to myself even easier. I'm not interested in spending time with people, mostly because they cause anxiety to perpetually pound inside me. The nerves created insecurities and embarrassing misunderstandings when I was little so it became natural to distance myself.

Soon enough, everyone thought I was some sort of freak.

I never bothered correcting them because they're right.

I'm a fucking loser weirdo.

What started as awkwardness morphed into fury, but only toward myself for being this way. It's all my fault.

At least now everyone at school pretends I don't exist, but their taunts behind my back carry across the echoing classroom. The snickering ridicule and cruel names bounce directly to me but all I do is hunch down further.

I don't blame them for keeping quiet to my face. Considering I'm built like a professional linebacker and barely eighteen, I'd turn the other way too. I work out almost constantly to manage my anxiety and ensure the threatening madness doesn't take over. Probably doesn't help that I never talk to anyone or even look their way.

But why the hell would I?

Everyone I cross paths with has only offers sneers.

Except her . . .

If no one else was around, I'd talk to Lennon. She can have all my words and focus. I'll give her anything she asks for without a moment of hesitation.

She quickly peers over her shoulder and smiles at me again.

What does this mean? Does she like me? Or is she secretly mocking me like everyone else?

Not sure I could handle the latter.

I'm used to being alone and planned to continue this way until a certain girl plowed into my life. The moment Lennon strolled into homeroom and sat in front of me, the whirlwind in my mind settled and she was all I could see. I don't understand my powerful reaction to her. Maybe I never will. What I do know is Lennon has given me a sliver of peace and reprieve from my shitty reality. Even if she doesn't know it.

The dismissal bell rings and everyone begins shuffling out of the classroom. I stay in my seat, unable to comprehend the attention Lennon gave me. Even when she gets up and leaves, I'm paralyzed by the rare joy rushing through me. It evaporates without her presence and the familiar dread slams down on my shoulders. My stinging eyes clench shut as I count the hours until our next class together. Only two today—I can survive that long.

After scooping up my stuff, I begin the lengthy trek to next period. This damn school is so big they give us ten minutes of passing time but it's still not enough. Luckily kids get out of my way, making room in the squished halls for me to pass. My long hair acts like an extra shield while I keep my gaze averted but their whispers hit my ears.

Hulk.

Weirdo.

Loser.

Stupid.

Crazy Eyes.

The last one has stuck through the years, but I don't know why. Apparently, my idiotic peers have an issue with my blue stare never settling on anyone for long. I've been told the color is strange—very light blue blending into a darker edge—but the shade doesn't seem odd to me.

Fuck them for judging me.

But I always get them back.

I gladly return the favor by hacking their social media accounts. It's easy to make a mockery of them with a few clicks of the mouse. They screw with me and I fuck them back harder. All from the comfort of my own home. Everyone thinks I'm dumb but soon they'll realize how wrong that assumption is.

I keep walking without another thought, ready to get away from all these bodies. I'm uneasy and restless as fuck but thankfully get separated from the masses when I head downstairs.

As I'm passing the cafeteria on the way to gym, I hear a faint cry coming from a darkened alcove on my left. My stride falters momentarily as I wonder what's going on but it'd take a lot for me to get involved. I plan to keep going until *her* voice rings out.

"Please let me go. *Please!*" Lennon's whimper echoes across the small space and slams into me. I easily recognize her delicate lilt and immediately cross the short distance separating us.

Jason Hicks, a well-known asshole around campus, has Lennon shoved up against a door in the shadowed corner. At first, it's difficult to see what's happening but as I approach it's clear he's lewdly thrusting his hips into her. Lennon keeps begging him to stop but he cuts her off with a snarl.

"Shut the fuck up and stop struggling. You're a damn tease, Lennon. It's time you pay up for tempting me and I expect you to meet me after school this time. Otherwise we'll just ditch class together now. Your choice, babe." His disgusting words ricochet around the secluded area.

I'm right behind them but only Lennon notices me. Her usually tan complexion is ghostly white as tears stream down her cheeks. Her blue eyes widen and plead with me to do something, *anything*, to stop him.

Any awkward discomfort disappears as anger seeps into my veins. My words rumble from deep in my chest, "Leave her alone."

Jason's head tilts to the side and he glances over his shoulder. He snorts loudly while glaring at me. "This doesn't involve you, Crazy Eyes. Get out of here and go back to being a silent weirdo, like you're good at." His disgusting mouth twists into a sneer.

The familiar nickname grates on my already fraying control and my body trembles with the desire to wipe the arrogance off his face but I hesitate to use my strength against someone. I'm standing motionless, waiting for Jason to go away on his own, when Lennon breaks the silence.

"Please." Her angelic gaze bores into me. "Help me." Her tone is meek but to me it sounds like a scream. She needs me and I'd never deny her anything.

My hand automatically reaches out to grip Jason's neck with bruising force, my fingers digging deep into his flesh. In the next breath I yank him back before shoving him to the side. He bounces off the wall before stumbling into the empty hall.

"I told you to leave her alone," I growl at him.

Jason's jaw grinds as his stare ricochets between Lennon and me. "Fuck off, Ryker. She's my girl and none of your business."

"I want nothing to do with you. I'm not your anything," she quietly mutters behind me.

"You're going to get it, Lennon. Just wait." Jason barks but his lips clamp shut when I take a few steps toward him.

My chest tightens as I imagine what his threats could mean. Flames lap at my skin as I allow the fury to take over. "If you ever bother her again, you'll be dealing with me. Got it?" My throat burns as I force the words out.

The untamed anger must show on my face because he doesn't respond again. With a final scowl at me, Jason trudges away and out of sight. I've never unleashed the aggression that's constantly festering within me on someone else but he'd fucking deserve a real beating. I attempt to cage the roiling hate bunching in my muscles with a few deep breaths. I'll have to push myself even harder at the gym tonight but it's worth it. Anything involving her is.

As the red hue fades from my vision, tingling awareness settles in and the telltale nerves start flooding my system. We're all alone. Lennon is behind me and I'm just standing here.

I slowly turn around and find her cowering in the corner, her guarded gaze searing my soul. Her shoulders shake as she sniffles and horrible possibility strikes me.

Fuck, did I scare her?

That's the last thing I want so my feet shuffle back to put some space between us. The horrible taunts begin echoing in my mind, even though it's completely silent around us.

Idiot.

Creep.

Loser.

Monster.

Freak.

Crazy Eyes.

Crazy. Crazy. Crazy.

My head twitches as I lower my stare away from her frightened features. "I'm sorry, Lennon. I didn't mean to upset you. He made me really mad though." A heavy sigh shudders from my chest. "I don't usually act like that." My voice is gruff from disuse but I get the point across.

I take another step back but her words halt my progress.

"Please, don't leave. You're not the one who scared me. You saved me, Ryker."

My eyes lift to her as I ask, "You know my name?" My heart starts pounding and I'm sure she can hear the rapid beat.

Lennon nods and smiles slightly. "Of course. I sit in front of you in three classes. Plus, you're pretty hard to miss."

Shame heats my cheeks as her words sink in. She's making fun of me, just like everyone else. I was stupid to believe she could see me differently, no matter how much I wish she would. Lennon is perfection and I'm a bumbling ogre so it shouldn't surprise me. The hurt splashes me like acid and my entire body burns as I move further away.

"Where are you going?" She suddenly blurts while stepping toward me.

I shrug and glance at her, drawn to her. I can't find the words to explain my feelings though.

She inches closer. "Did I say something to upset you?" Her hand reaches for me and I flinch, afraid of what her touch will do to me.

"I'm used to it. Everyone calls me names." I manage to choke out, even though my mouth is desert-dry.

Lennon's face scrunches up in an adorable way as she asks, "What? I don't get it."

"You said I'm hard to miss, as in my size. I get it. Very funny." Embarrassment slithers up my neck and causes me to turn away further. "I'll see you around, Lennon." My tone is flat and lifeless.

My plan to escape disappears when her palm settles on my back and everything inside of me freezes.

"Will you wait a second?" Her whisper reaches deep into my chest and squeezes. "I didn't mean it like that, Ryker. Really. You're hard to miss because, umm, well . . . I think you're cute." She giggles and my knees almost buckle. That tinkling laugh mixed with her touch turn me into a sloppy puddle of mush. It's like my brain is short-circuiting and all functioning is jammed so I remain completely still.

When I don't respond, Lennon takes her hand away and the

loss cramps my stomach. I'm floundering, unsure of what the hell to do now. My anxiety threatens to consume me the longer we're silent and I'd rather not have a panic attack in front of her. Thankfully she saves me from deciding.

"Can you turn around? Just for a minute?" I do as she asks, as though I'm locked under her spell.

Lennon stares at me with a look I can't quite comprehend. A dimple dents her cheek as she grins at me. "I really appreciate you helping me with Jason. He's such a jerk and has been harassing me since my first day. Maybe he'll leave me alone now." She exhales loudly and bites her bottom lip. "What can I ever do to repay you? I seriously owe you one."

My mind scrambles for something to say but I'm horribly distracted by her aqua eyes focused on me. I clear my throat before muttering, "You've given me plenty already."

Lennon's eyebrows bunch in confusion as her head tilts slightly. "Huh? Why do you say that? I haven't done anything. You're the savior around here." She chuckles lightly while fidgeting with her shirt sleeve.

Okay . . . Shit.

I shouldn't have said that. My brain swirls with explanations to smooth this over so she doesn't think I'm a freak. I decide to be honest. "Your smile is all I need."

That's exactly what she gives me before dipping her chin. "Wow. That's really sweet." She gazes up at me from under her long lashes and the impact is detrimental to my pulse. Having Lennon's completely undivided attention on me is similar to being electrocuted. The high voltage seems to zap through me, stealing any coherent response, so I continue gawking slack-jaw like a creep.

Lennon sighs while her eyes scan my face and I wonder what she sees. She shrugs before saying, "I'm going to the office and telling the principal what happened. Do you wanna come with or go to class?"

I don't like either of those options but my regular schedule appeals to me far more than being questioned by the principal. Leaving Lennon stabs at my chest but the thought of sitting in the office makes my skin crawl.

"Will you be all right alone? I should probably get to class but if you want me to come with, I can." I'd go with her no matter what, even if my heart seized with panic, but she's already shaking her head.

"This isn't my first rodeo so don't worry." She starts edging around me so I step out into the hallway. "So, I'll see you around?" She asks while backing away.

I nod while tracking her retreating form, regretting the safer choice of going to class and separating from her. I'll be seeing her *very* soon though.

Lennon waves before blessing me with another smile, which is exactly what I need to calm the worry slithering through my veins. She turns and walks toward the stairs while my mind conjures up imagines of her being attacked again. Next time could be worse and I can't allow any danger to reach her. I wait a few beats before following, the need to ensure she's safe settling deep within me.

No matter where she goes, I'll always follow.

one

LENNON

I dream of stormy waters, thrashing and turbulent, crashing against the unsuspecting shoreline. The waves are relentless and chaotic, refusing to calm. Over and over, again and again, without rest. Whenever I wake, it's always to images of him.

~ Four Years Later ~

"GAH, STOP IT. YOU'RE EMBARRASSING me." I elbow Lucy, my pesky roommate, in the ribs as a blush burns my face. My eyes dart around Brewed Awakenings, the café near campus, before pinning her with a glare. Hopefully no one heard her crude comments.

Lucy rolls her eyes. "I'm trying to help you out, Len. You're always complaining about not meeting enough guys." Her eyebrows wiggle while her chin juts toward the cute boy ahead of us again.

Just thinking about approaching him has cramps attacking

my legs. "I'm too shy and awkward. I can't just force it, ya know? Urgh, of course you don't know. Flirting is automatic for you."

She snorts as I point out the obvious.

"Whatever, Luce. You know it's true so don't bother denying it. Things are different for me though. Talking to a man shouldn't make me feel uncomfortable but it does. The right guy won't make me nauseous and ready to panic though." My voice tapers off as familiar humiliation surges through me.

"Don't put so much pressure on yourself. At our age, dating should be easy and breezy. Just for fun." Laughter paints her tone when she nudges me lightly. "The fear won't suddenly vanish unless you start doing something about it. Like ripping off a bandage. Just walk up and introduce yourself. He seems completely harmless." Confidence radiates from her and envy bleeds from me.

Lucy has been giving me a similar version of this same speech since we met freshman year. No matter how many times she's lectured me over the years, I'm still single and a total novice when it comes to the opposite sex. I wish there was one solid reason to blame but my lack of experience is a messy hodgepodge, starting with my parent's rigid upbringing. It didn't help that my family frequently moved when I was growing up or that my naturally introverted personality beckons me to blend in the background.

I can't leave out the painful truth that a few of my interactions with men involved the explanation of *no means no*. Perhaps my passive attitude causes some misunderstanding but I never asked for the slobbering attention those jerks gave me. Thankfully something always interrupted them before any real damage was done. The most memorable was a certain blue-eyed boy I'll never forget.

Before my thoughts get whisked away by Ryker, the line

we've been waiting in shifts forward and it's my turn to order. I grab my usual hazelnut coffee and toasted Asiago bagel before finding an empty table.

"So, what do you think? Is he worth a little case of the jitters?" Lucy asks once we're seated and digging into our food.

I scowl at her after sipping my favorite caffeinated blend. Her words are almost enough to ruin the sweet flavor lingering on my tongue but not quite.

"Knock it off. It's so much worse than that and you know it. We've been over this how many times? I can't just stroll over there and start up a conversation. No way."

"But what if he's an amazing catch and you're letting the future walk away by not giving him a shot?" Lucy's brown eyes are pleading but she won't change my mind.

I take another bite while making a noncommittal noise.

"If he was someone special, I'd know."

"Like your secret admirer?" She sing-songs before smirking.

My skin prickles at the mention of the mystery person who's been leaving me random gifts since I started college. I almost choke on the lump in my throat while trying to respond.

"Probably not. If he or she actually liked me, they'd show their face by now. There hasn't been anything more than the usual coffee and bagel for a month anyway. Maybe they're finally realizing I'm a waste of their time."

Her slim brow arches at me.

"You honestly believe that? Yeah right. You're such a sap and I know you love those little surprises. Most people would have thrown that stuff away, afraid of being drugged. But you gobbled it up after reading the cute little note. I enjoy that trust about you, even though it freaked me out at first." Lucy admits while jutting out her chin. "It's obvious you've got some odd connection with this person. It's gotta be killing you not to know who it is. Can't we try tracking whoever it is down yet? We can ask anyone who works here since the coffees and bagels are always from here."

I'm already shaking my head before she finishes.

"Nope. I've told you numerous times it's more exciting not knowing. It's whimsical and sweet and meant to be treasured. I'd hate to discover their identity and be totally disappointed for whatever reason. I like fantasizing much better."

I release a slow breath and think of the last larger package that arrived, perfectly wrapped in sunflower yellow paper. I picture a chiseled jaw clenched in concentration as thick fingers work carefully to fold the edges just right. His light eyes sparkle in the lamplight and crinkle in the corners when a smile lifts his lips. I image him reading a steamy scene from the autographed romance novel he delivered to me. Another soft sigh leaves me.

"Yeah, it's definitely better to keep it a mystery."

Lucy grunts.

"But it's been happening for years. *Years,* Len! And it's gotta be a guy. What girl would keep up the charade for this long? We're far too impatient for that."

I shrug.

"We'll probably never know and that's just fine. Pretty soon I'll graduate and move on. They won't know where to send stuff anymore."

The idea of not receiving those items makes my heart hurt. I'd never admit it to Lucy but I look forward to getting them. Far too much based on the storm cloud that's suddenly rolled over me.

"Why do you look so upset? Considering you don't care enough about this person to find them, right?" She asks warily.

"Or did someone mess with your coffee?"

Not wanting to tell her the entire truth, I circle back to a safer subject.

"Nothing really. Just sad Mr. Right hasn't shown up yet and I'm kind of lonely."

"What about the guys in your classes? Don't you ever talk to them?"

I groan in annoyance.

"Only because the professor tells us what to say. Plus, most of my courses lately are in the design studio and unfortunately those men are interested in something I can't offer." My disgruntled tone has Lucy snickering.

"Let me hook you up with someone!" She huffs when my head shakes wildly back and forth. "Seriously, you're going to be a virgin forever. You can't leave college without giving it up. Just think of all the sweaty fun you've already missed out on."

"Says who?" I question with a raised brow, very familiar with this topic.

Lucy releases a frustrated squeak before practically yelling, "Me!"

My *shhh* is immediate and thankfully her tone dials down a few notches.

"I care about your lady bits and honestly worry about the obvious neglect their dealing with. Don't you have urges, woman?"

Even though the last part is whispered, my gaze darts around in fear that someone heard.

"I can't believe you just said that. Why are you always concerned with my supposed needs? Luce, you get enough action for both of us. I'm fine living vicariously through you."

"Yeah, I see that." She exhales heavily. "Sorry for getting on your case. *Again.* It's just difficult for me to understand since my parents didn't hide me away. In a way, it's sweet how dedicated you are to finding the right guy to steal your virtue." Lucy's sympathetic eyes contradict her sassy tone. Deep down, I know she understands me.

My friend thinks waiting for love is old fashioned and maybe I am. There's nothing wrong with wanting a man to actually care about me before sharing my most intimate pieces with him. I'm not saying we need to get married first but being wooed and spoiled a bit isn't asking much. I refuse to believe romance is dead, so I'm fine holding out until my heart pitter-patters.

I want the butterflies, dammit.

I've had the fluttering eruption deep in my belly once before, which only strengthened my resolve to find love. Next time, I want the boy to return my affections because being ignored by the only one I craved sucked ass. Other than him and the random package deliveries, my body has remained tingle-free. Imagining anyone else giving me that type of reaction hasn't been possible either.

So, here I am. Twenty-two and zero experience with guys.

I've chatted with men online after Lucy encouraged me to set up a dating profile. I even met a few for a date but it never went farther than a rushed meal. Each time they ran off scared, like something was chasing them away. It had to be me, right? After several failed attempts, I was the only common denominator. Plenty showed interest but I never got to know any well enough to try.

I'm not totally unfortunate looking, at least according to Lucy. She says my light eyes pop against the dark color of my hair, making a sexy contrast. Her words, not mine. It must be my introverted nature, but that's not something I can easily change.

I've always been on the quiet and skittish side, frequently getting stuck in my mind while trying to figure out what to say. Whatever tumbles out of my mouth ends of being a mash of consonants and total gibberish. My date would laugh and I couldn't hear myself think over the rapid beat in my chest. By the time they realized I wasn't worth the trouble, my nerves were completely shot and frazzled.

A loud snap in front of my eyes yanks me back to the present.

"Earth to Lennon." Lucy is giving me her typical expectant look—a cocked brow paired with a squint. "Where'd you disappear to in that head of yours?"

I rub my face while clearing the clouded thoughts away.

"Sorry. I got caught up in the disastrous whirlwind called my life—the usual stuff. My parents called earlier asking when I was moving back home. Can you imagine?" I almost gag at the idea. "Where am I going to live though? You're leaving me." My lip sticks out in a pout and Lucy mirrors my action.

"Will you be alright while I'm in Paris? I feel terrible leaving you." Her eyes mist over a tad as her voice takes on a note of concern.

Discussing Lucy's extended stay overseas causes dread to slither up my spine. My best friend will be an ocean away for months. I won't ruin the experience for her though so I force a small smile.

"Don't worry about me. You're the one leaving home. Who knows what kind of trouble you'll get into over there."

She rubs her hands together while practically bouncing in the chair.

"I know, right? That's the best part. I have no idea what to expect and the possibilities are endless. Maybe I'll meet an amazing man who wants to make all my dreams come true." Lucy's brow bobs obnoxiously.

Worry strikes me like a whip.

"Promise to come back?"

She scoffs.

"Of course, Lenny. Or you'd move over there with me."

A loud snort shoots out of me.

"That's rich. As if my parents would survive just thinking about it. Nah, I'll stay put and you'll be back soon enough."

"What are your plans?" She questions before popping the last bite of bagel into her mouth. My forced exhale says it all. "That bad, huh?"

I rest my chin on my open palm while trying to keep the stress bottled up.

"Just a lot of work. I really need to start selling more clothes if there's any chance of opening an actual business. My professors are allowing me to keep working in the studios through the summer but I'll need to find a new space by fall. I have a few solid months to create a bunch of inventory but then what?" My frustration whooshes out in another heavy breath. "There's no way I'll ask my parents. They'll wear me down until I agree to come back home. One day at a time for now."

Lucy's forehead scrunches as her soulful stare sears into me. "Len, should I stay? For real. I can go to Europe next year. Let me help you get started."

"No way, friend. This trip is the jumpstart to your career. I'll survive, like always. Plus, you'll be a phone call away." I hope my words don't expose the nerves crawling up my throat.

"And if you need me, I won't hesitate to come home. You know that, Lenny. Don't be afraid to tell me."

"I won't. Promise." It comes out as a whisper and I straighten up and attempt to infuse my system with confidence. "I've been selling almost everything posted on my site. I'm not sure but it seems like the same person keeps buying from me. They're local too so shipping doesn't cost a fortune. Everything will be fine."

My sweet friend smiles at me.

"All right, if you say so. I'm still expecting a few crop tops to drive all the French men crazy."

I laugh while nodding.

"The more skin showing, the better. I'll have you decked out in all the latest trends before you leave."

"You're the greatest, Lenny." Lucy reaches for my hand and gives it a quick squeeze.

If only I could get a man to feel the same way.

two
RYKER

SHE LOOKS SO BEAUTIFUL, JUST like each time my eyes devour her.

Lennon's long hair whips around as she begins vehemently shaking her head. I image her turquoise eyes are more green than blue right now, the bold color thrashing like a tumultuous sea at whatever crazy idea Lucy is suggesting.

As I watch her in the café, sitting with her snarky friend, my body practically vibrates with the need to get closer. I never do though. A safe distance separates us and I always remain hidden from her sight. Even though Lennon is everything to me, she isn't aware of my constant presence. I'm not sure she ever will be.

I take a sip of coffee and contemplate the reality I've

created—my purpose set in stone after that unexpected day four years ago. A shudder rolls through me, even after all this time, as I imagine how differently that incident in our high school hallway could have ended. If I hadn't been passing by at that exact moment. If Lennon hadn't cried out for help. If Jason dragged her out of earshot. The horrible possibilities are endless. All those reasons, those potential threats, are why I'm always here for her. Just in case she needs me.

Well, if I'm being honest, I need Lennon just as much. Probably more. She makes me feel . . . better. My entire life before her, I was isolated and alone. When Lennon showed up, she altered the secluded path I'd been traveling down. Because of her, happiness flows inside of me and constantly warms my chest. There used to be overwhelming darkness but her sunshine has given me patches of blinding light. Sometimes a ghost of a smile teases my lips as I bask in her glow. On a few rare occasions, I've actually experienced flutters in my gut and it's fucking weird when that fluffy stuff floats through me.

My phone vibrates, effectively yanking me from the blissful moment. I scoff while reading the message.

Dx8MM: Get your ass online.

My fingers fly over the touchscreen, easily shutting his ass down with a quick reply.

AATS: Not home. I'll be around later.

Dx8MM: You're getting lazy only working at night. Help me something quick.

AATS: Screw off. I make more money in a few hours than you make in a week. Even if I could help, I'm busy right now.

Dx8MM: Watching out for your girl?

AATS: Always.

Dx8MM: She know yet?

AATS: Didn't I tell you to screw off?

D doesn't respond to that, which doesn't surprise me. He's aware of my situation with Lennon, even though he only knows the bare minimum. D is the closest thing I have to a friend, and that's using the term very loosely. Not like I'll ever meet the guy or know his real name. We became virtual partners by accident after I blocked him during a hack. He tried busting through my bulletproof firewall for big name corporations rich enough to pad my pockets. I caught D in the act and shut his ass down, which still makes him salty. He's smart as fuck and a total code wizard but no one is better than me.

Falling into the hacking world was a natural transition since computers have always been easy for me. What started as a hobby, and great way to fuck with bullies, has turned into a cash-cow. I make money by cracking into a company's interface network system and prove I can provide impenetrable security. There is always a way, no matter what they're currently using to keep me out. It's my job to create impossible firewalls that even I can't tear down. These huge businesses hire me to protect them from . . . well, me.

I glance down at my phone and scroll through a few emails. My fingers tap on one from a new contact and my eyes narrow at his bullshit ramblings. They all like to bark demands and expect immediate results but I'm the one pulling strings behind the scenes. It's mind-boggling how naive some of these people are when it comes to current security programming. Wealthy assholes hire some two-bit crook to install a flimsy anti-virus software and believe that's all it takes to be safe from hackers. If I'm feeling generous, I send an email letting them know how easy it would be for me to steal their money. If not, I royally fuck their shit up. I'll plant some backward binary code that breaks apart some vital pieces of their entire structure and causes complete chaos. I leave a blatant trail so they contact me for support. It helps with the boredom when Lennon is sleeping or in class.

Dick move? Absolutely.

But they deserve it for shoving their heads in the sand.

This is my version of sticking up for the little guys who can't defend themselves. I might not be the one behind a fancy desk, wearing an expensive suit and barking orders, but the power resides in my fingertips. With a few clicks of the keys, their whole world could be ruined and I'd be standing victorious in the rubble. Luckily, these people are eager to work with me so I don't have to truly destroy them. Sometimes it's fun to think about though.

Even to my warped mind, this all sounds twisted as hell.

Living in virtual reality almost one hundred percent of the time hasn't helped with my unusual social habits, especially stalking Lennon. I've been building an empire while watching her every move. Everywhere she goes, I'm able to follow while my bank account busts at the seams. It's easy and convenient considering my true interest is keeping her within my sight where I know she's safe.

As I look back into Brewed Awakenings, every man seems

to glance Lennon's way. She never seems to notice, completely oblivious to her appeal, but that suits me just fine. If she was interested in constant attention, I'd have a lot more work to do. I've only had to face off with a few jocks that thought Lennon's refusal was optional but that could easily change. Usually guys are easily dissuaded after a few online threats. I might be the size of a tank and prepared to fight but social anxiety still plagues me.

She starts laughing and my ears burn with the desire to hear the melody bubbling from her. Jealousy squeezes my throat. I should be the one sitting with her, making her crack up, or maybe even blush. Instead I'm watching from the sidelines and she's completely unaware of my existence.

Why can't I go in there and say hello?

That would be expected from a guy interested in a girl.

Why can't I be normal for her?

Lennon needs someone worthy of her pure light. Why would she settle for me? I toss my empty cup away and blow out a long exhale, trying to push away the dark clouds closing in. Nothing will take her sunshine away from me, even my own demeaning thoughts.

She stands from the table to leave and I track her graceful movements. Lennon is everything perfect, even her stride is careful but confident. Never a step out of place, which doesn't surprise me considering her gaze tends to be downcast more often than not. The long flowing dress she's wearing, one of her creations, swishes along the floor and it reminds me how tiny she is.

My hands clench in effort not to reach out and do . . . what? Touch her? Hold the door open? Silently stand frozen in front of her like a loser?

The latter is precisely what would happen, despite the

desperate desire thrashing through me. My fingertips tingle as I imagine her soft, silky cheek against my calloused skin. Suddenly my heart begins pounding an erratic rhythm as my pants grow tight—something that only happens when Lennon is involved. Everything within me aches for her—mind, body, and soul—so these reactions no longer surprise me. All I am always craves all of her.

Perhaps it's time to leave another present. Something bigger than the usual coffee and bagel I drop off several times a week. I open the browser on my phone and check her updated website bookmarks. My eyebrow arches while I scan through several pages for sewing machines she's recently visited. Looks like I found exactly what she wants. I tilt my head while reading a few reviews, trying to decide on the perfect model.

I always try finding the items Lennon's searching for so her reaction is extra special. A few months ago, I gave Lennon a book she'd been trying to find. My memory of the smile that lit up her face makes it seem like yesterday though. Her joy was worth the extra effort of tracking down the elusive author. Compared to that guy, I'm a social butterfly.

A snort rolls out of me at my form of a joke, even though no one is around to listen. I'm not normal when it comes to communicating with others but Lennon motivates me to fix my deficits. Only for her though. Everything I do is for her. Always.

And I wouldn't change a thing.

All right, that's a blatant lie. There's a ton I would change about this twisted arrangement—the first being Lennon's unknown participation. It would be nice to walk alongside her rather than two steps behind. I've become the creep everyone called me. In my defense, it's for her protection.

But far more than that.

Keeping her safe provides me with a convenient excuse to constantly follow her, and invading her privacy is part of the gig. It's not socially acceptable for me to constantly be watching her through the window. Deep down I understand hacking into her accounts isn't right. I realize stalking Lennon isn't either but I've tricked myself into believing that she needs me to watch over her.

Right?

Wrong.

Even my crazy brain can admit it's far more than keeping her safe. This is greater than needing her light to warm my freezing skin. I love her in an all-consuming way and there's no way to control the tidal wave of emotions constantly thrashing through me. My feelings for her are molded into my soul and spirit, like vital pieces I can't live without. I was already obsessed during our senior year but since then, it's become an unstoppable need. Every muscle in my body seizes up while considering the probability of her rejecting me. Lennon saved me from the wreckage by offering genuine compassion, and I'll never forget it. Even if she wants nothing to do with me, I'll forever be in her debt for changing my life.

Most importantly, I want her to be happy.

Lennon wants to start her own business and I'm determined to make that happen. My eyes return to the phone screen as I check the ads for her website. I've got three running currently and they're performing quite well. By the looks of it, her inventory is completely sold out. I close my eyes and picture her stunning smile when she saw these results. The pressure in my chest eases but worry still worms through me.

What's the chance this ends with us together?

My brain suddenly switches gears, shutting down those wayward thoughts and I slip my phone back into my pocket, as Lennon and Lucy exit the café. I pull my hood up farther, making sure my face is hidden, as they pass by along the sidewalk. They'll be heading back to Aire Gardens—their apartment building—before Lucy goes to class and Lennon heads to her studio as always. They're giggling again and desperation quickly claws at me. I continue trudging along behind them, just out of sight, and consider a time when things might be different.

A cool breeze hits my face and I squint against the morning sun. A subtle smile lifts my lips, which still seems foreign but has become more common lately. Thinking of Lennon next to me, aware of my existence, gives me a glimmer of joy. Can she forgive me for all I've done wrong? For every bad decision made with decent intentions? Hope blooms in my chest that Lennon will understand my quirks and odd behavior. Fear of rejection lives inside of me, the inevitable downfall once she discovers the truth surges through my veins. I'll take whatever chance there is, no matter how small, that Lennon can accept me. My desire to be better for her has been powering through me like oxygen in my lungs. When we see each other again, I'll be a different version of myself than she remembers. One she'll hopefully be able to love.

My palm rubs over the hood covering my shortly cropped hair while I wonder if Lennon would even recognize me. A lot has changed since we last saw each other. I've been trying to become more comfortable in my skin. Sometimes I still shake my head, expecting the thick curtain of hair to fall across my eyes. But my longtime defense against cruel leers is gone and has been for a while. When I face Lennon, her eyes will be on me and there won't be anything obstructing her view. I need her to see me, all of me, so she realizes I'm offering everything to her. *Forever.*

When we arrive at their place, *our place* since I live in this complex too, the girls jog up the front stairs while whispering about who knows what. Their chatter doesn't interest me at the moment. I'm watching Lennon's subtle curves sway under her dress and a groan is begging to release from my throat. It takes all my might to keep the primal reaction trapped but I fail epically.

Lucy suddenly glares at me over her shoulder before muttering, "Creeper."

The nasty barb is familiar and rolls off my tense shoulders. I'm well aware that lurking behind them is suspicious as fuck but also don't care what Lucy thinks of me. My only interest is Lennon's opinion of my presence.

As if hearing what I'm waiting for, Lennon shushes Lucy before turning my way. I lower my face slightly but am able to catch the clear shock covering her features as her gaze scans my broad frame. Her posture stiffens as her aqua pools swirl restlessly. My cheeks blaze under Lennon's direct attention and nerves begin bubbling in my gut.

What's she's focusing on most?

My towering height? Wide shoulders? All black clothes? The features I keep hidden?

Sweet coconut fills the air and I breathe deeply, desperate to inhale her scent. A rumble rises from my throat.

She smells so damn good.

Lennon's breath hitches and the knuckles clutching her bag turn white. Everyone is terrified of me, but is she? Based off her reaction, most would say yes, but they don't watch her like I do. If Lennon were truly terrified, she'd already be locked inside the apartment, safe behind a closed door. Instead, she continues standing before me. Just staring silently.

Why?

These questions hound me more than anything else. The curiosity eats away at me, even more so lately, so I've found myself becoming bolder. This isn't the first time we've been in this situation, almost close enough to touch yet the distance seems like a gaping hole. Desperation gnaws at me to close the gap.

I've been getting more reckless on purpose because of this frenzied desire, like I want her to catch me. In high school, we had a chance but it slipped away because I was too chicken shit to pursue her.

I won't make those mistakes again.

If Lennon gives me reason to believe she wants to know who I am, there's no backing down. She never sees my face so she isn't aware who's beneath the hood. Sometimes I wonder if she senses I'm always around. When she glances out her window or peers around the corner, does she know it's always this dark stranger watching over her? I'm usually out of direct sight, except instances like this but . . . maybe she finds me familiar for some reason.

What would happen if I lowered my shield and showed her who I am? Would she be scared then? Or would she be happy to see me?

What would happen then?

The unknown grates on my already fraying nerves.

Four years is a long time to wonder. My fingers twitch as I think about pulling the hood down. I could start with my face . . .

As I'm considering the options, Lucy huffs loudly and jerks Lennon's arm. I want to snap at her for being rough but the demand lodges in my throat. Talking to her isn't possible and the potential of revealing my identity dies off with that reminder.

The time isn't right. Not with Lennon's friend here and all the people walking by. We need to be alone, somewhere quiet, where I have an actual chance to speak up. I'll keep waiting because this isn't something that can be rushed. Our reunion will be special.

Lennon's gaze is still locked on me. Even with my chin dipped to stay hidden, I see her light eyes boring holes into the shadow created by my hood. I'm getting lost in her all over again until Lucy pulls her further away. "Come on, Len. We gotta go." She whines loudly, effectively snapping the last lingering tendrils of the moment I'd been trapped in.

I take a few steps back to head for the back entrance. Lennon shakes her head, as if snapping out of a haze, before focusing on her friend. She clears her throat before murmuring, "What did you say?"

My heart rate kicks up as I imagine her distracted because of me. My feet falter before freezing in place, taking one last look at the beauty standing near me.

I'm going to impress her one day—at least that's what I keep telling myself. I've been coasting along, biding my time until we can be together. It seems like the time could finally be right but the ditch I've been digging is damn deep.

Will she be able to forgive me?

I won't focus on that right now. My sunshine just graced me with her attention and I'm going to bask in the warmth before the chill seeps back in. Today has been good.

Another hint of a smile tilts my lips as I secretly track Lennon's movements inside the lobby.

See you soon, Sunshine.

three

LENNON

I'd give up all the stars in the sky to stare into those stormy waters again. Even just for a moment.

I HUM ALONG TO THE swoony country tune playing on the radio as my fingers continue layering silky fabric on the mannequin. The soft blue material reminds me of a cloudless sky and I imagine a classy woman wearing the dress to a fancy garden party. She'll eagerly show off the effortless draping and perfect pleating between the subtly different shades that make up the cascading pattern. The slight peek-a-boo effect swoops down and around before smoothing out along the hip. No one wants extra fabric there, especially the glitzy bombshells I'm hoping to sell my creations to.

Dream big, right?

A frustrated puff escapes past the pins held between my lips.

I secure a loose fold with steady fingers while reining in my overzealous mind. It's easy for my thoughts to wander while I'm working but now's the time to start getting serious. Before I get lost in the possibilities of the future, my pieces need to be marketed.

Too bad I suck at selling my product—no matter how much love and passion bleeds into each stitch. Lacking confidence is a career killer, especially in the saturated field of fashion design. I'm a dime a dozen unless I step the eff up and put myself out there.

In the real world, it doesn't matter that the professors rave about my unique style and intricate attention to detail. My portfolio is packed full of specialty pieces that exceeded their standards but that won't matter if I don't start promoting. By some stroke of luck, customers managed to find my website and purchased the clothes I've listed. I barely made a profit but getting any sales at all was a huge accomplishment. The chances of that continuing to happen without proper advertisement is very slim.

Getting my brand on the map isn't the only hurdle I need to clear. Thinking about losing this fantastic workspace twists my stomach. Everything piling up is a migraine waiting to happen.

I take a deep breath as my gaze sweeps across the sprawling green campus from the floor-to-ceiling windows near my station. My thoughts begin drifting again but this time I'm distracted by visions of a particularly mysterious man wearing a black sweatshirt. I begin wondering who is he and what he was doing following us earlier. Chills race up my spine as I recall his intense presence silently standing before us. The panic and fear that typically attacks me around men didn't crash down. I pondered my odd reaction, or lack thereof, the entire time my eyes devoured his broad frame. The short moment reminded me of another time with a different boy, the only one who brought comfort.

I focus on the crowded sidewalks, picturing him out there somewhere. Was he following us? Could he be the one I've spied nearby during those moments when my intuition bangs like a steel drum and my skin prickles?

I first noticed a looming figure in dark clothing several weeks ago. The suspicious person seemed to be hanging around one second then vanished the next. Those instances were eerie as hell, and always sent flashes of alarm skittering through me, but I managed to brush them off. At first, I considered a connection to the random gifts from my "secret admirer" but that seemed like a crazy assumption. My wild imagination, plus the pesky paranoia instilled by my strict parents, are probably to blame.

My eyes roll in frustration as I refocus on the project in front of me. I bite my lip while quickly glancing outside. The enormous man from earlier could be watching and excited tingles spread through my stomach just thinking about it. What would he see? Me—being lame as always—woodenly working away. Maybe I should make it more interesting for him? Just in case he happens to be out there?

What am I thinking? He could be a super creep, waiting for me to put my guard down so he can snatch me. But that doesn't seem right, even though I can't explain why.

Am I completely wacky for having this strange attachment to a figment of my imagination?

Yes. I'm losing it. I shouldn't be pining after him and attempting to draw male attention to myself. An involuntary shudder works through me as I recall unwanted hands wandering over my skin. I lick my dry lips while remembering my voice cracking with desperation. Men can be serious schmucks.

I scoff while shaking my head. My fingers push a few more pins in place as I get back on track. There's no need to spend more time worrying over shit I can't control. End of story.

A fast-pace song begins, the rhythm easy to bop along to, and my hips start naturally swaying to the beat. All the stress and possible what-ifs start fading away as I get lost in my design. I really get into the groove while singing about saving a horse and riding a—

"Nice moves you've got there," a masculine voice calls out.

I release a startled squeak as I spin around. My chest rises and falls with rapid breaths as I gape at the unexpected intruder.

"David. Holy shit, you scared me. What are you doing here?" My words sound like a rattling wheeze as I attempt to rein in the shock.

He chuckles lightly, as though my reaction amuses him.

"Don't look so scared, Lennon. I heard the music and wanted to see if it was you up here. Figured if it was, I'd try prying you away for that drink you promised me last week."

I inwardly groan at the reminder of my commitment to going out with him. There's no way I'm going anywhere with him alone—just the thought makes me queasy.

"Uh, I'm pretty busy today. Now isn't a good time, David. I really need to finish these looks and get them posted online."

He steps closer and my heartrate ratchets up at his proximity. We're totally isolated in this part of the building and my mind spins with possibilities of escape. David keeps moving further into the room until he's hovering at the edge of my workspace. My vision swims as I scan the surrounding area, frantically looking for a way out.

"Come on, Lennon. Don't turn me down again. I'm taking

you out, just one drink. Let's go." David isn't asking and his forcefulness cranks my anxiety up another notch.

My feet instinctively stumble backward when he stalks closer. His putrid cologne assaults my nostrils and I swallow several times to avoid throwing up. I shake my head violently while trying to keep him in sight.

"No, thank you. I have a lot to get done. I think it's best if you leave now. Please." I have to force the words from my tight throat. My voice is meek and matches the quivering havoc in my chest.

David lewdly licks his lips and says, "You don't really mean that. Let me help you with . . . *everything*." His eyes flash and a bolt of terror stabs me.

This cannot be happening again. Please, not again.

Suddenly a shrill noise breaks apart the uncomfortable stand-off. I quickly snatch my ringing phone off the table while keeping a careful eye on David.

Saved by the fucking bell.

"Hello?" I practically yell, eager for an excuse to get the fuck out of here.

"Hello, is this Lennon Bennett?" The sweet feminine tone wraps around me like a fuzzy blanket.

"Yes, this is she."

"Hello ma'am, I'm a representative calling from AmeriBank. You have a credit card through our federal union. This call is to inform you that there's been some significant spending on your account that we've flagged as suspicious. Do you have a moment to review some recent charges?"

What? Suspicious spending? This can't be possible. My credit card is only used in emergencies—

"Ma'am? Are you still there?"

I swallow my panic with a loud gulp. "Yes, I'm here. Sorry but I've never dealt with this before. When did these charges take place?" My shoulders tense in preparation of hearing the worst.

"They started coming through over the past few days. If you're near a computer, we can look at the purchases I am referring to. Is that possible, Ms. Bennett?"

My eyes clench shut as I think of the nearest options. There are a few study carrels upstairs with desktops. That will have to do.

"Yes, I have to go a different room but it's not far." I'm already on the move but a hand on my arm stops me.

The unwanted touch adds another chaotic layer to this swirling fiasco and I'm about to lose my shit. I glare at David and wrench my elbow from his grasp. I'm done with his bullshit and continue walking.

He pipes up as I'm exiting the door, "This isn't over, Lennon. You owe me a date."

I roll my eyes and keep going. He can wait forever because it's never going to happen. I reach the stairs and start huffing my way up.

"I'm almost to the computer. Sorry for keeping you waiting. I'm thankful for your call," I rasp into the phone after clearing the second flight.

"It's part of my job, Ms. Bennett. We strive to ensure our customers are protected. We appreciate your business."

Tears prick my eyes at her gentle pitch, like a balm soothing my jagged nerves. She hasn't said anything monumental but her slight reassurance is exactly what I need to hear. Too much has been stacking up lately and today took a sharp turn for the worst with stupid David.

There's one computer available as I approach the alcove and

my knees almost buckle in relief. I send up a silent thank you to whatever lucky stars exist for this tiny gift.

"All right, I'm getting there now. Do I just sign into my regular account?" I ask while rounding the cubicle edge.

The woman mutters softly before speaking up, "Ms. Bennett, it appears the suspicious activity on your account was a false alarm. The recent purchases suddenly cleared and your balance has returned to zero. I greatly apologize for this inconvenience and any disruption my call caused."

I stumble into the wall as my mind plays catch up. "What? How is that possible?"

"It depends on several different factors, Ms. Bennett. In your case, considering the charges are already gone, our processing team must have already caught them as fraudulent and stopped payment. I recommend double checking your account tomorrow to be sure everything still looks normal. If anything seems unusual, please don't hesitate to call us back. Is there anything else I can help with for now, ma'am?"

My scrambled thoughts swirl out of control. "Uh, I guess that's all for now. If you say it's all right. I don't understand any of this but I'll keep an eye on my balance. Thanks for your help." I expel all the air in my lungs while hanging up the phone, glad this was an apparent false alarm.

I move toward the empty chair to process the past thirty minutes, and check my account just to be sure. Before I'm able to sit down, my body locks up tight. Sitting on the desk next to the keyboard is a very welcome pairing—a wrapped bagel and large cup of coffee. All the tension bleeds out of my frozen limbs as I collapse on the seat. I don't understand why this unknown person and these unexpected surprises cause my heart to sing with relief.

I do know they couldn't have chosen a more appropriate time to drop off my favorite goodies.

A single sob hiccups from me and there's no stopping the tears this time. Once I read the attached note, on the usual yellow post-it in a familiar bold script, my emotions get the best of me.

When Lennon laughs, the clouds part and sunlight streams through. Every worry fades away. Is it possible to bottle the sound and play it on repeat?

I PEER AROUND THE HALLWAY corner and blow out all the pent-up panic from the last hour. I take a few deep breaths to loosen the knot currently squeezing my chest. That was a close fucking call. Far too close for my liking.

My eyes strain as I stare at Lennon curled up on that uncomfortable chair. The tears streaming down her cheeks make it very difficult to keep my distance. Every instinct is screaming at me to comfort and love her. I take a hesitant step forward, uncertainty warring with driving need, when Lennon sniffles loudly.

And then she smiles.

I slam to a stop as the radiant expression stretches her plump lips. I shift closer, as if pulled by a force beyond control, but am still hidden behind the adjacent cubicle. Lennon's delicate fingers trace my note on her coffee cup.

Is that smile because of me?

Is she happy because of the treats I left?

Could she be wondering who I am?

I can't start wishing for miracles like that but . . .

This was the exact reaction I'd hoped for. I figured she could use her two favorite treats after pouring hours into creating another beautiful dress. I'd been looking forward to basking in her sunny warmth while she discovered the goods outside the studio door. Those moments keep me sane.

And he fucking ruined it.

When I found him hounding Lennon, murky red spattered across my vision. This dumbass had bothered her in the past and he received a fairly pleasant warning from me. Too bad he couldn't fucking stay away. I'll be paying him a special visit for that stupid choice. My fists grind the concrete wall as my eyes narrow into slits. No one messes with my sunshine and gets away with it.

While my mind is spinning with ruthless possibilities, Lennon starts eating her bagel. Even from my hiding spot, I can hear the soft humming noises she makes with each bite. Watching her enjoy something I provided temporarily cools the fire burning in my gut. She's here, safe, and almost in reach. Exactly where she belongs.

The vibration on my wrist pulls me back to reality and I tamp down a groan from being interrupted.

> *Dx8MM: Account back to normal. His phone signal has left the building so he should be long gone.*

I tilt my head back and blow out a heavy breath, thankful to have help with this clusterfuck. I pull out my phone and send a quick reply.

AATS: Appreciate it, D. Owe you one.

Dx8MM: Next time I ask for help, day or night, you better pay up.

D probably won't let that go until I actually return a favor but he saved my ass tonight. The online life I've built comes in handy when I need a quick hack.

My forehead thumps into the rough brick pillar before I roll my brow against the abrasive surface. Fuck, this is one more mark against me that I'll have to explain to her someday. Will she understand my motives? What about my insane infatuation with her? How could she ever excuse some of the shit I've pulled? I better keep hoping for a damn miracle.

Why can't I be normal?

Can she love a flawed man?

I'll never deserve her perfection.

What I've been doing all these years is an unspeakable invasion of her privacy. I can't stop though. She's sunk deep into my soul. So deep she'll never escape. I can only hope that once Lennon knows, she'll want to stay. My devotion to her is what keeps me going—it's who I've become.

I wouldn't exist without her.

Lennon stands from the table and stretches. My hands burn in need, itching to rub her sore muscles. She's so beautiful, even with slightly swollen eyes and blotchy skin. Those temporary imperfections make her more stunning to me.

When she turns away, I manage to move a bit closer without her noticing. My body zaps awake with her close proximity. It's becoming increasingly difficult to stay away when everything within me begs to give in. I won't hold out much longer.

Lennon's several feet ahead as we go downstairs. When she takes a sharp turn and heads outside, it becomes obvious she isn't returning to work tonight. Hopefully we're heading back to the apartment where she'll be safely tucked away for the night. My eyes focus on the gentle sway of Lennon's hips as she slowly walks along the path. Everything else fades away as I get lost in her hypnotic rhythm.

Being around Lennon's light, even from a distance, has been repairing the painful damage from my past. After leaving high school and all those assholes behind, my anger has been slowly dissipating. The heat boiling my veins had become a constant onslaught so when the flames started fading, I wasn't sure how to handle the shock to my system. Without their continuous jeers and jabs, the raging fire seems more like dying embers.

Obviously, there are certain situations where Lennon has been around guys and they're beyond my control. I keep my shit in check while she's in class or working on team projects. I can't block her from all communication with the opposite sex but there's definitely a line they aren't allowed to cross.

I've gladly scared off the idiots who thought there was a possibility for more. It's usually fairly easy, especially since Lennon steers pretty clear of men on her own, but there's a stupid few who refuse to take a hint. My strength and bulk come in handy when additional intervention is necessary—anxiety be damned.

As we near our building, I shove all the grit away and pay attention to the beauty shining in front of me. Lennon's pace seems more lax than her typical stride and I wonder why she's moving slower than usual.

Is she avoiding something at home?

Maybe Lucy has a guy over. I grit my teeth at the thought as the evening air cools my heated face.

Maybe she's considering going back to campus to finish her blue dress. But what about Douchebag David? He might be waiting around regardless of what D's tracking suggests.

Lennon looks over her shoulder and I dodge from her sight, but not fast enough. My distracted brain missed her subtle change in step and she probably caught me. Again. But after a slight pause, Lennon continues moving like nothing out of the ordinary happened.

She hops up the front steps and unlocks the door without another backward glance. In the next breath, she's dashing away to her apartment and I'm stuck outside with a muddled mind. Watching Lennon disappear is like a punch to the gut, just like every night before this one. I'd love nothing more than to stand outside her window and process the baffling events from today but there's another stop to make.

After pulling out my phone, I get to work finding David. With a few quick swipes, I've tracked his cell signal and my eyes hone in like a heat-seeking missile. He's conveniently located a few blocks away at a bar. Probably the place he wanted to drag Lennon off to. The idea of her being forced out with him is enough to ignite a fierce explosion of fury in my blood. The anger consumes me as I stomp the short distance to him. My entire being surrenders to the madness surging through me, which evaporates the momentary bliss that was comforting me.

I send a decoy message disguised as one of his regular hookups—I uncovered her identity ages ago. "Molly" wants to meet at a club across the street, and David, being the pig he is, will gladly accept a chance at getting laid. My lip curls as I imagine his reaction to discovering me instead of a drunk co-ed.

David shoves through the door a moment later, a cloud of vomit-inducing cologne accompanying his disgraceful strut. I almost choke from my spot along the alley wall but spit rage instead.

"Hey, Asshole." The growl vibrates from my chest.

David stops in his tracks and whips around, a sneer marring his features. "Who the fuck do you think—"

His bullshit rant cuts off when he steps closer and catches sight of who's speaking.

Little bitch is scared, my mind silently taunts.

I hear him gulp as his eyes widen to saucers. David clears his throat while raising his chin, as if suddenly realizing fear is wafting from him. When he squares his shoulders and straightens his spine, I almost laugh. He'll never be half my size but his efforts are entertaining.

I move away from the cool brick against my back, ready to get this shit settled. "I tried to warn your stupid ass before but that clearly didn't work. Now you've pushed me beyond reason and forced me to waste precious time dealing with you." My words spit through clenched teeth, the rage threatening to bubble over.

"What the hell are you talking about?" David sputters loudly.

When I begin crowding his space, his lips clamp shut.

"You don't mess with another man's woman. That's how you get the shit kicked outta you. Didn't anyone ever tell you that?" The venom leaks from my voice.

David holds out his hands, as if that will stop me from getting closer. "Dude. You've got the wrong guy. I didn't touch any girl who's attached."

I scoff loudly. "Stop lying, Pinocchio. I can see clear through your bullshit. You haven't just been messing with mine either. Don't wedding vows mean shit to you? What about school policies or the fucking law?" My fists clench tight, desperate to punch him, but I deliver a different blow instead. His dark eyes blink slowly but otherwise he's frozen. "Since you're not getting the hint, let me make it easy." I carelessly toss a few snapshots of him and Professor Carter by his feet. "And I've got plenty more where those came from."

He peers at the images and I swear his face drains of all color. "Who the fuck are you? What the hell is this shit? You're spying on me?"

"You done with the twenty questions? Seems pretty clear what's going on to me. These don't leave much to the imagination."

"You're a psycho creep. Need to watch me to get off?"

"I wouldn't spew that shit my way. You're a despicable piece of shit, preying on vulnerable women. Don't bother twisting the truth." My harsh tone bounces off the building wall and I almost hope people hear me.

David puffs out his chest. "What the fuck is your problem?" He shakes his head when a savage sound breaks from my mouth. "Never mind, don't bother answering that. Just tell me what you want."

"Leave. Lennon. Alone." Each word is a sharp command.

His face scrunches up while he glares at me. "Lennon? Lennon Bennett? What the fuck? She doesn't have a boyfriend. That sweet honey—"

I launch at him and he stumbles back against the wall to avoid me. "Don't you dare finish that disgusting sentence. Lennon is none of your concern. Hear me? Leave her the fuck alone or those pictures will be plastered all over campus. Got it, Dickhead?"

"Fuck. You're a special case of crazy." His cold stare locks on me, looking for what I don't know. "Fine, what the fuck ever. I'm not dealing with this shit. She ain't worth the trouble."

I slam my hand against the wall, roughly bending his ear in the process. "She's everything to me but *nothing* to you. Don't talk to her. Don't look at her. Don't even say her name. Get it through your thick, dumb skull. Lennon is mine."

"Fine. *Jesus.* Back the fuck off. I'll leave her alone." His gaze drops with the last word.

I take a step back, my roaring fury easing with his acceptance. "Don't make me find you again. I won't be so nice next time."

David's head snaps up. "And you'll get rid of the pictures?"

My lips curl in disdain. "We'll see."

five

LENNON

HE'S BECOMING REALLY OBVIOUS.

The mystery man is here again, hidden in the shadows and out of clear sight, but I'm catching onto him.

After noticing him standing behind me the other day, the dark stranger has been appearing everywhere lately. I'm pretty sure this guy wants to get caught. Perhaps he's been hanging nearby a lot longer and I'm just realizing it. My pulse beats wildly, the whooshing pounding in my ears as I continue watching him. This reaction isn't from fear but rather a startling awareness of his recurring presence. I'm not scared of him, though most might be, and the need to know why snakes through my system.

We've been playing an intense game of hide-and-seek since

that afternoon outside Aire Gardens almost a week ago. I'll go somewhere—my studio, Brewed Awakenings, around campus, my apartment—and after settling in, begin searching for him. He's always there, waiting to be spotted. Each time I find him, my belly tightens as a smile lights up my face. Discovering him out there, lingering in the background, has become something I really look forward to.

Why didn't I notice sooner?

Perhaps it's my total inexperience with dating, and the opposite sex in general, that has me getting far too attached to these moments. I'm getting wrapped up in the fantasy of him, of what he represents. This stranger—Seek is what I've started calling him—is the closest thing to a boyfriend I've ever had. I find myself daydreaming about him, wondering who he really is, when did he find me, and most importantly—why me?

I press my palm flat against the cool glass and stare at him leaning against the large oak tree outside the Student Center. My thoughts are becoming more and more consumed with a guy I don't even know—at least not really. Yet it seems like I do.

Seek is wearing all black again, just like the other times I've found him lingering. The leaves and grass are bright green so his dark form is easy to spot. My eyes scan the busy campus and discover people are avoiding him. Even though the paths are cramped, everyone gives him a wide berth. I tip my chin and wonder if he prefers it that way. He doesn't appear to want attention from others but what the hell do I know. My faces inches closer to the glass as I wait for him to address someone.

It's as though he's existing without really living, physically present without planting roots. Seek is like a shadow.

His face is completely hidden by a hood so I can't gauge his expressions or reactions to what's going on around him. Seek's broad shoulders are almost wider than the tree trunk and his height towers over most passing by. Maybe they're afraid but I'm not.

I know plenty about wanting to fade away from certain situations, as if I'm not here at all. The burning attacks my lungs when a man approaches, painfully stealing my breath. Why can't I be invisible in those moments? Then creeps like David can't see me. Maybe that's why I find Seek so quickly—I know the best spots to hide.

But not from him.

I like that he sees me and appears to know where to find me. I'm aware of him too. Does that make me weird? Either way, I've been different my entire life so one more reason won't tip the scale.

Guilt pinches my gut as the confusing connection between us appears to grow stronger. Since moving to Webster and starting college, I've only experienced this calming sense after receiving a gift from my secret admirer. I thought that was something special but Seek has me all mixed up.

I glance down at the note from this morning, written in the same bold script on the familiar yellow post-it.

I've saved each one. My wooden box at home is almost stuffed full with golden notes. Each one contains a short message from my secret caffeine and carbs supplier. The messages frequently reference the shining sun, warmth and light, smiles and laughter, or moments of joy. Sometimes the subject isn't so happy, like black paint splattered against a white canvas, which makes me wonder about his mood in those moments. In one short sentence, they convey so much.

The words swirl through me as my fingers trace the letters. I contemplate the identity of the sender, wondering who's behind these notes. These presents are from a person with a tender heart and romantic soul. Someone I hope to meet one day. Very soon.

My eyes lift to Seek and my wild imagination takes off at light speed. How crazy would it be if the two were connected?

The idea first popped into my mind when I thought Seek was following behind me after the terrible incident with David. When I'd subtly turned around, someone darted off the path before I got a decent look. Did he see what happened in my studio? Or maybe who left the coffee and bagel at the study cube? Exactly at the right moment? How else would my secret admirer know unless they'd been watching me . . . much like Seek is now.

There's no way they're the same person. But that doesn't stop me from wondering.

The prodding urge to approach him pokes at me again. As I gaze at Seek's downcast head, I wonder what would happen. Fear holds me back. The potential backlash of breaking the silence and closing the distance separating us hums through me like a warning but the need to know more about him bangs louder.

I jump what has to be five feet in the air when Lucy whispers in my ear, "What are you looking at?"

My heartbeat skyrockets as I force myself to turn away from the window.

"Luce, give me some damn warning next time. You scared the shit out of me."

She rolls her eyes and pops out her hip. "If you weren't staring like a creep, you would have heard me coming. What's so interesting out there?"

"What do you mean? I was just looking at the grass finally turning green," I mutter, trying to avoid her interest, but I should have known better. Lucy doesn't let anything go.

"Liar. Just tell me or we'll watch together until I figure it out. Like one of those hidden image games at the bar." She smirks at me before peering outside.

I cross my arms, as if protecting my heart from a brutal blow. "The guy is back. The one who wears all black." My voice is soft and barely there.

"The weirdo that follows us? Why are you staring at him? He's freaky as hell!"

My hackles rise in defense as I practically growl, "Seek is not a freak! Don't call him that."

"What did you call him? Oh, no. No way. You gave him a nickname? Do you like him?!" Her brown eyes widen as her jaw hangs.

"I don't even know him. But he . . . intrigues me."

"Are you freaking serious? You're terrified of all men except the scariest one of all. His size alone is enough reason to tuck tail and run." She glances out the window in his direction. "I mean, look at how big he is. His shoulders are almost as wide as the tree trunk!" Lucy's tone goes shrill at the end and I wince before peering at her.

"*Stop it*. You're judging him. We don't know anything about him other than he hangs around a lot of our frequent stops. He's probably very nice." I sigh in exasperation, my fuse shortening by the second.

Lucy scoffs. "Why are you defending this dude? He's been stalking us for who knows how long. Don't give me that nonsense about it being coincidence. He's probably planning—"

"Okay, seriously. Knock it off, Luce. You watch way too many crime shows. He's done nothing wrong. Maybe he likes you or something." The words taste bitter on my tongue and a sharp throb stabs at my chest.

She shakes her head wildly. "Uh huh, yeah right. I should go out there and give him a piece of my mind. If he's not following us, it sure as hell seems like it. If he's interested in me, I do not appreciate his wooing strategy. He needs to find somewhere else to hang out."

"No!" I squeeze my eyes shut for a few seconds. "Let's just leave him alone. Seek is harmless. He never gets close enough to be considered threatening. I actually think he's helpful."

Lucy looks at me with a blank stare, as if she can't believe what I just said.

"What the hell are you talking about?"

I bite my lip while deciding how much to share. "I'm pretty sure he was around the night David was harassing me." She motions with her hand for me to keep going. "I told you about the bank calling with the false charges, but there's more. I saw someone wearing black in the alcove and he might have followed me home. From a safe distance."

"And why do you think it was him?" She juts her chin toward Seek outside.

I nod slowly. "Guess what else? When I got upstairs to the

computer, there was a coffee and bagel waiting." I scrunch my face, waiting for her ridicule.

She gasps. "Like *the* coffee and bagel?"

"Yeah," I say slowly. "I'm not sure what to think. It's a weird coincidence, right?"

Lucy stays quiet for a few beats, cranking up my nerves. "You can say that again. Seems like both are trying to protect you." She sighs before saying, "That's twisted but also really sweet. I'm not sure how to really feel about it." She tilts her head slightly while staring at me. "Now I really want to ask him what the hell he's doing."

"What? No. No, no, no. Can't we just wait and see?"

"Until what? He makes a move? Seek, which is a ridiculous name by the way, looks very comfortable against that tree. What if he keeps this weird shit up for years without revealing his identity? Then you'll have two big question marks."

I drop my gaze to the floor. "I know," I grumble.

"So, let me go ask him. What's the worst that could happen?"

"He could leave." My heart stutters at the thought.

"And? What would be so bad about that? It's not like you're getting to know him from here. Besides, I'm not confident he's stellar crush material." Lucy reaches out and touches my arm, squeezing gently. Her gaze is warm and comforting but her words sting.

Another cramp attacks my chest.

"There's something about him, Luc. I don't know what it is or how to describe it other than he's calling out to me. For years, I've been slowly getting attached to my mysterious gift giver. How could I not? And now that I'm assuming who it could be, my unexplainable attraction is stronger. Seek already means something to me, no matter how crazy that sounds. I don't want that to end."

She raises a questioning brow. "Okay, wow. I didn't know you had all that trapped inside you. He's only been around for . . . what? A week? I can try to be more supportive. Maybe. There's so much you seem to be hiding. You won't even share the notes with me," Lucy whines while flicking the paper still clutched in my palm.

"They're private," I whisper while glancing outside quickly. Seek is exactly where I saw him last but his head is no longer downcast. It seems like he's looking right at me. A shiver races up my spine as a decision settles in my gut. "I'll go to him."

Lucy chuckles but stops suddenly when she catches my serious expression. "I'm sorry, what? You're going to talk to him? *You?* The girl who refuses to speak to any guy? I don't believe that for a second."

"He's different. I'm not afraid of him. I think he's been waiting for me to notice him." Lucy is the one hearing my words but they're spoken for Seek. "I'm ready to meet him."

"When? Like *right now*?" She almost yells the last part and I shush her without taking my gaze off Seek. "Len, look at me."

A heavy sigh deflates my shoulders as I force my eyes to hers.

"This is serious, Boo. Regardless of your freaky intuition or whatever, that man could be dangerous. If you're honestly going to approach him, I'm coming with you. No arguing."

My lips twist in thought. If Lucy tags along, she'll understand what I already know about him. Plus, she has a way of calming my crazy. Even though Seek doesn't make me nauseous or ready to bolt, I'm full of uncertainty.

I nod while agreeing, "All right. Let's go."

"Dude. Slow down. We should make a plan. What if he pulls out a weapon when we get too close?" Her sharp tone has my spine snapping straight.

"It's broad daylight, Luce. You're being really paranoid. I don't see what the big deal is."

"That's exactly the problem. Your self-preservation is totally whacked. And that's why you have me." She smiles wide, pride shimmering on her face.

My own lips lift in a small grin as I shrug my shoulders. "It's time for me to be risky, especially because it feels right."

She sighs before saying, "You win. I guess this is happening. Right now, apparently."

"Yes. I'm ready." I tell her for the second time. My head twists back to the window as I silently prepare for what's about to happen. Seek is still there, waiting and watching.

Lucy remains quiet beside me, looking toward the mysterious man too.

Hopefully not a mystery for long . . .

six

RYKER

When the sun is shining directly in your eyes and nothing is visible but blinding light, what else is there to do but bask in the glowing warmth?

I'D FORGOTTEN WHAT IT FELT like for Lennon to acknowledge my presence—this week is proof of that. My body and soul had been hibernating since the last smile she gave me all those years ago. But not anymore. Every part of me has lit up like a Thanksgiving parade since she's looked my way again.

Right now is a perfect example as Lennon continues staring at me from the big bay window of the Student Center. I rub my clammy palms together while trying to stop my heart from exploding. Her gaze on me is a shot of adrenaline and I've lost any ability to control the electricity buzzing under my skin. The current zaps along every inch, from my skull to my toes, but the shocks aren't painful. I consider them sparks that rapidly spread until all of me is consumed with blistering heat.

After years of freezing alone, I welcome the burn.

My hungry eyes eagerly devour every gorgeous inch of her behind the glass. Her long brown hair floats around her, a dark halo capturing the sun. Lennon's teal irises glisten and sparkle, full of awareness and intelligence. They crinkle at the corners as a small smile lifts her glossy lips and my knees threaten to buckle at the sight. My gaze swoops down to check out the flowing dress she's wearing, the warm spring weather allowing her to show off more skin than usual.

I realize that secretly following Lennon all this time had been slowly tangling my mind. The memories of her focused on me seemed vibrant but compared to this reality, they'd faded. Somewhere along the line, it became satisfying to watch Lennon from a distance—silently making sure she was protected. Our interactions were one-sided as I stalked behind from the shadows or tracked her location on a computer screen. I'd tricked myself into believing that was enough for me, so long as I was near her.

Until now.

Everything has changed since Lennon caught me following her and shifted that turquoise gaze my way. I'm a junkie, an addict, for the soaring high Lennon's attention gives me. I want it all the time and there's no alternative—her warm rays of light and lakeshore eyes are the only cure. So, I get closer and closer—bolder and bolder. There's no going back to hiding in dark isolation. I'm ready to bask in the stunning sunshine while swimming in the aqua sea.

Lennon turns away from the window and walks toward the exit with Lucy. It's Thursday, which means the girls will grab coffee from Brewed Awakenings before going to class. I push away from the tree and roll my stiff neck before moving closer to the sidewalk. When my eyes settle back on Lennon, I stumble back as cold fear lodges in throat. My heart takes off at a breakneck pace as she walks down the path.

Straight. Toward. Me.

What the hell am I supposed to do?

Expletives run through me with the beat of my rapid pulse. Even though it's logical to assume she would approach me, if even just to tell me off, I didn't think she would. Or at least not yet. Panic ripples through my gut and I desperately search for a way out of this unexpected twist. I'm not prepared for her confrontation and the urge to hide scratches at me, like a persistent pest that won't go away.

She's getting even closer. There's no doubt about it—she's planning to confront me. Oxygen isn't properly passing through my clenched chest and I'm getting light headed. Maybe if I pass out, she'll forget about me stalking her.

While attempting to remain conscious, against my better judgement, I focus on Lennon gliding my way. Her toned legs bring her closer and I get lost in the smooth stride. Lennon is like the mirage I've imagined shimmering in front of me countless times but this isn't a hallucination—she's real and this is actually happening.

My fists jab deeper into my pockets while I try getting a grip on the panic crashing into me. My resolve to stay standing here starts to shatter. The instinct to flee claws at my gut, begging me to escape, but the desperate craving for Lennon's attention wins and my feet remain cemented in place.

She stops several feet away and I suddenly realize she's not alone. Lucy's presence will make it impossible for me to speak, not that words were very likely in the first place. But I'd make an attempt for Lennon. *Only* Lennon.

I watch her sandaled feet shuffle while her fingers knot together. My mind focuses on the jerky movements and I wonder if this means Lennon is nervous. The potential of us feeling the same way eases my overwhelming anxiety slightly.

Until she speaks.

"Are you dangerous?"

My gaze snaps up at her quiet words and everything within me tenses painfully. Just the mere thought of her considering me a threat has my soul screaming in agony. Lennon stares back at me with wide eyes, her mouth in the shape of a tiny o, and I want to ask what these expressions mean. Is she worried? Surprised? The need to shout that I'd never hurt her burns my throat but the words don't form.

I wildly shake my head instead, silently pleading that she comprehends my meaning.

Lennon clears her throat softly. "I didn't mean to just blurt that out but it's important to know. You wouldn't lie, right?" She tilts her head while studying me, quietly assessing the risk level no doubt.

Lucy scoffs but I don't pay much attention. From under my hood, I watch my beautiful sunshine as her aqua gaze sears into my hidden face. An involuntary shudder rolls down my back before I nod, eager for Lennon to believe me.

"Will you talk to me?" Her request is a soothing melody to my frazzled mind but I can't do what she's asking. Not with Lucy around and all these other people passing by. Regardless, desperation slices into me and I want nothing more than to give Lennon all the words spinning through my brain, especially when a small smile tips her lips, as if she's inviting me to speak . . .

But I can't shove a single syllable past my clogged windpipe.

I slowly shake my covered head and the encouraging grin falls from her lips.

"Oh, all right." She pauses for a moment. "But you're responding so . . . just yes or no questions?" Lennon's voice is calm and warm, taking the chill from my bones. My heart gallops with hope that she wants to know me.

My chin bobs hesitantly as I wait for what happens next.

When Lennon takes two steps forward, everything else fades away and my system floods with molten lava. She's still out of reach but within my orbit, and I definitely take notice. I'm always cold so wearing a hoodie in the balmy weather never bothers me, but it does now. The need to strip off my black armor clangs within me but I shove it away. Sweat gathers on my brow as I'm exposed to her direct sunlight. The overwhelming heat sucks all the air from my already starving lungs.

Lennon distracts me when she asks, "Are you following me?"

I contemplate my response for a moment, trying to decide if being honest will scare her away. At this point, there's no use denying it. I cautiously nod again before holding my breath.

She sucks in sharply and her eyes flutter shut as a delicate hand rests against her neck. My stomach sinks like a boulder without that connection to Lennon, the bright attention she gives me, and my intention to stick around wavers. Her chest shudders with a shaky breath before her bottomless pools open and I'm drowning in those depths once again. I'll never leave if she keeps looking at me.

"I want to ask why you're watching me but that isn't something you'll answer. Let's see . . ."

When she bites her lip and a groan rattles from me, Lennon jerks back. Fucking primal shit is going to ruin this for me. My throat spasms with an apology but before I try forcing out words, she steps forward and hovers on the edge of my personal space. Lennon straightens her shoulders and lifts her chin before whispering, "Do you like me?"

Once the words pass her lips, I watch a rosy blush blossom on her cheeks. The bright color lights up her face and I want more. I lick my lips, ready to force the answer from my mouth. Her question deserves a proper response and my jaw ticks open—

"Can we see your face or what?" Rings out from behind Lennon.

My guard slams back down with the blatant reminder of Lucy's presence. I'd been so wrapped up in sunshine that it appeared we were alone out here. *Big* mistake.

I grit my teeth as the obscenities begin silently flying for everything happening at once. At Lennon for choosing now to ask something like *that*. At Lucy for being here and making matters a thousand times worse. At myself for being a shy mute who can't string a few sentences together when it really matters.

Lennon seems to sense the change and she moves into my personal space. I shift my face to stay hidden while she tries to repair the damage her friend caused. "Hey, don't listen to her. She only came along because she was worried. But I'm not. I understand if you don't want to take off your hood. It's okay. Don't take off, alright?" Her velvet murmur wraps around me and draws me back into her light.

My fingers strain to write the words my mouth can't say. I suddenly remember the note in my pocket for later. I was planning to include it with a coffee delivery but now will be better. My hand snatches the small square and I ignore the cramp seizing my muscles. The yellow paper vibrates as I slowly show it to Lennon.

Lennon gasps and covers her mouth with a trembling hand. Her quaking fingers reach out to grab the note.

"It's you?" Her question is barely there. "Oh my God, I've been wondering about you for so long. I can't believe . . ." Her quivering voice tapers off as her glassy orbs lift to my shadowed features. My heart stalls when a short sob escapes her and the need to provide comfort cascades over me.

But I don't know how.

A single tear slides down her cheek and without much thought, my thumb brushes it away. Lennon's breath hitches before a blinding smile stretches her lips. "It's you," she says again but as a statement this time. A small grin lifts my mouth automatically, mirroring her joy the best I can. Lennon can't see all of me and in this moment, I wish she could because my reaction belongs to her. She doesn't know who's masked by the sweatshirt yet seems to accept my shield. She is standing here *with me* as happiness leaks from her features.

Maybe it wouldn't be so bad to hope.

While she stares at my darkened face, I gaze into her sunshine, and we just . . . enjoy the moment, basking in one another.

I hardly notice this time when Lucy pipes up. "All right, guys. This has been super fun and not at all weird but Lenny, we're going to be late for class."

My eyes never stray from the light in front of me but she's leaving. A pinch of panic prickles at me but she'll be safe, as always.

Lennon smirks and an adorable dimple appears. "Thank you, for everything. I'm so happy we've finally met. Well, I talked and you listened but whatever." She waves a hand in front of her before continuing. "Anyway, this was . . . good. I gotta go but will you find me later?"

I nod while silently saying, *"Watch me follow."*

seven

LENNON

WHY DID I BOTHER COMING to class?

As the professor drones on about our seminar presentations, all I can think about is Seek and what happened earlier. Shock continues to creep through me, even hours later. It's surreal to finally discover who's responsible for delivering the yellow sticky notes and gifts after all this time. The secret that's been following me for years has been revealed. Well . . . kind of.

I haven't seen Seek's face under the hood but hopefully he'll show me soon. Maybe there's a reason he's been keeping his identity a mystery, but I want him to trust me.

This entire situation is wild and unexpected, yet I'm calm and ready for more. Mostly because receiving his undivided attention is extremely thrilling. I'm not sure my heart rate will ever return to normal. Does this make me naïve and gullible? Maybe, but I've never been risky. To me, Seek is worth taking a chance. There's a gut feeling deep inside that's telling me he's special.

My lips lift into a dopey smile as I recall the note he just gave me. As I reach into my pocket to touch the paper, my eyes slide shut.

I want to be his sunshine.

His romantic messages have kept me floating in bliss and I want to know what else he's capable of. I want to see it all, hear his words, and hopefully Seek will let me.

Why is he holding back?

Goosebumps prickle my skin while I stare out the window, getting lost in visions of his mysterious features. His strong, square jaw jutted out from the shadows. The light skin was covered with dark stubble and my fingers twitch at the memory, wanting to feel the texture. Would the hair be soft and silky or scratchy and rough?

Seek's full lips were also exposed to my hungry eyes. I saw them lift into a barely-there smile when we stood close together. I pictured the rest of his face transforming with the expression and longing shot straight to my core.

Is his nose sloped or straight?

Are his cheekbones high?

Does his forehead crinkle when he's concentrating?

Every piece of him interests me but the feature that claims most of my attention is the color of his eyes.

No matter how hard I try steering my imagination away, light irises appear like a flash in the night. The unique combination of ice-blue fading into midnight navy always left me transfixed.

That stunning shade is impossible to forget.

I blink slowly while getting dragged deeper into the crystal-clear depths, once so familiar to me. His thick lashes would flutter shut, like dark clouds protecting the bright sky. Suddenly the boy from my past forms completely, watching me from the sidewalk. His broad build radiates strength, similar to Seek, but Ryker is my original pillar of wonder.

I've tried forgetting him but he's always in the back of my mind. He's the only guy I've found a connection with, no matter how silent or one sided it was. Four years have trickled by since those ocean eyes sucked me in but my dreams always remind me. Ryker is long gone and I let him get away.

My gaze gets misty and I wipe the moisture away. When I glance back outside, a figure on the sidewalk has a black hood covering his head and the memories of Ryker evaporate. Seek is the one actually here, in the present, and it's time to move forward.

"Ms. Bennett?

My instructor's voice startles me from the daydream.

"Um, y-yes?" I stutter quietly as my flickering gaze focuses on her.

"Care to join the class? Or will you be staring out the window all period?"

My cheeks heat with the shame of being caught.

"Sorry," I mutter before she turns away.

My hand gets busy copying the notes on the board while the professor moves forward with the instructions. She discusses the final project guidelines and I quickly glimpse at the outline she's scrawling across the board. I write barely-legible notes so my attention can return to the intriguing scenery beyond these stuffy walls.

As I glance back to the sidewalk, Seek's dark form is gone. Disappointment sinks like a brick in my stomach but his disappearing act is for the best.

This weird fascination is becoming more distracting and my concentration needs to get back on track. Graduation is less than a month away and my priorities can't take a backseat while I chase this random guy around. My Seek-crazy heart almost convinced my usually levelheaded mind to blow off class altogether and I never do that.

I could have stayed there, staring at his darkened face, all day if Lucy hadn't pulled me away. She told me one of us needed to be responsible after shoving me in the general direction of my first class. A muted snort escapes me at the thought of her being the dutiful one. That's hilarious. If anyone enjoys ditching, it's that girl. Lucy was just uncomfortable with the situation. I appreciate her watching my back and keeping my head screwed on straight.

Being impulsive isn't my thing—at all.

And yet, regret has been pooling in my chest since leaving him. Even the deeply ingrained devotion to my future career can't keep my thoughts away from him. What is it about him? I barely know this man aside from his beautifully written words and his peculiar habit of following me, but I'd skip out on my perfectly planned routine for him.

The afternoon drags by but I've finally made it to my last class. Without windows, the basement computer lab is like a concrete fortress with no escape. The knot in my stomach tightens as I weigh the options. My leg bounces restlessly as I contemplate leaving early. It's not like I'm really listening. My focus keeps bouncing between what happened earlier and what might happen later. With a heavy exhale, I settle deeper into the chair as stubborn determination wins.

There's no hope of catching sight of Seek down here so I'm doing my best to get some work done. My current assignment is to create a logo for a popular brand of Michigan-made kayaks. If my design is chosen, I earn a hefty sum to use for starting my own business, so this could be a huge win. I've been layering navy splotches mixed with black swirls until the entire screen looks like a midnight setting. The last thing a lakeshore company wants is a dreary symbol to dull their sparkle. I groan inwardly and rub my eyes before trashing the pitiful picture and starting over.

After choosing powder blue as my backdrop, inspiration strikes and I'm filled with newfound motivation. Soon bursts of yellow, orange, and red blend to create a magnetic image. My gaze gets lost in the rays blasting through the early sky.

The girl next to me leans over and mutters, "Dude. You're totally going to win. That color scheme is dope."

I offer her a small smile before returning to the screen and saving my progress. Finding my stride after that doubt is a hefty burden off my shoulders. This design is definitely the beginning of something solid and the final submission isn't due until next Friday. Having the prize money would make all the difference for me. A real chance to start my own company, *Len's Looks*.

When we're dismissed at the top of the hour I don't waste time sitting around but when I get into the hallway, my legs lock up without a clear plan of where to go. I've been obsessing about finding Seek all afternoon but completely forgetting to consider how.

I usually spend Thursday evenings in the studio since it's always quiet and abandoned. Other students are more interested in partying, while I see the night as open hours with no one around to bother me. Since the incident with David, I've been avoiding being alone down there but Seek will be around. I hope he will.

As I start walking toward the Art Center, my eyes naturally search the hidden nooks and crannies where Seek could be waiting. My mind floods with crazy possibilities as I contemplate what could happen. Everything inside my heart trusts Seek and wants to know everything he's willing to share. I'm very close to finding out. I can feel it within my bones.

My hand grips the door handle before I take a last look over my shoulder. I don't see him but that doesn't mean he's not there. Considering how long he's been delivering coffee and bagels without any hint of revealing his identity proves he's stealthy.

Where is he?

A heavy sigh deflates my chest when the space around me remains Seek-free. I head down the stairs and into the studio while keeping my chin up.

He'll be here soon.

He seems to know my schedule since he's conveniently parked in my path more times than not lately. There's no reason to doubt him now.

I don't see him but suddenly a scent from earlier floats in the air. With a deep inhale, musk and pine settle into my lungs while my lashes flutter rapidly. There's nothing artificial about the aroma clinging around me—it's just *him*. It speaks of days spent outdoors and nights in the gym. Seek has an organic smell that's not available in a bottle and after another whiff, my body is hooked.

And he's here with me.

Nerves squeeze my throat, forming a rock that makes it painful to swallow. My mind is swamped and it's difficult to concentrate.

I focus on the clench in my muscles and take a steady inhale to try loosening the tension. Everything about me screams anxious mess, which probably makes sense. There wasn't much rational thought going into this meet up in the first place.

Soft footfalls break up my chaotic musings and I'm grateful for the distraction. I'll drive myself crazy before getting a real chance to speak with this man. My sweaty palm rests on a nearby stool for much needed stability. I slowly twist around to face the guy who's been stealing all my brainpower. Air wheezes past my lips while waiting for his next move.

Seek's head is still covered and a shadow is cast over his face. I stare and remain frozen while he moves farther into the room after shutting the door. Awareness twitches in my limbs with him this close again, as if I'm tuned into his exclusive channel. I could normally watch him for hours and be content but in this moment, I'm ready for more.

My neck strains in effort but I manage to squeak out a quick, "Hello."

Seek's steps falter at my greeting and I notice his shoulders bunch up tight. My mouth gains a life of its own and begins spitting out randomness to fill the awkward stillness.

"I wasn't sure where to go so you'd find me. Then I realized you'd know where to find me, right? I mean, it seems like you've been around everywhere lately and this is a common spot for me. Plus, no one else is here. Not sure if you care but being surrounded by a lot of people isn't my favorite," I explain in a rush while my fingers fidget nervously.

After a few beats of tense silence, I prattle on. "Okay, so what happens now? Should we, umm, sit down?" My words are jumbled but I couldn't care less about that.

His trembling hands lift to the sweatshirt hood and slowly lower the black shield.

Holy shit, this is actually happening.

At first all I see is dark buzzed hair, cut close to his scalp. My pulse roars louder as he slowly lifts his face toward me. When the clearest blue eyes I've ever seen lock onto me, everything slams to a halt. I'm not prepared for the sight before me.

Could it really be?

"Hello, Lennon." His voice is raspy and hoarse but the words sear directly into me.

I gasp as the deep timbre vibrates my bones and resonates deep within my spirit. The ocean waves from my dreams crash over me and suddenly I'm drowning all over again.

As my knees give out and I stumble back onto the stool, my lips tremble with a name they've been desperate to say. "Ryker?"

> I like to picture us as two oddly-formed shapes that no one can decipher, but together, we create something magnificent.

WHEN MY NAME HESITANTLY SPILLS from her mouth, a mangled exhale chops out of me. I find myself once again stunned by her, but for a far more pronounced reason this time. My feet remain rooted in place yet a distinct tremor rockets through me. Every moment spent hidden in the dark, consumed by shadows, is worth it because of her instant recognition. White spots blot my vision as I replay her voice over and over.

Lennon remembers me?

She must but my congested brain is having an impossible time processing that fact. As her aqua gaze keeps flickering over my face, I stare back and catalogue the expressions taking over her features. Lennon's light eyes are blown wide open as her jaw hangs slack. Her nostrils flare with heavy breaths that I count to stay grounded in this moment. I'm sure she's surprised again, like when I revealed that yellow note earlier.

Even though I can't read people, I've studied Lennon. Knowing everything about her, from her favorite food to the variety of ways her lips tilt depending on her mood, is my only purpose in this twisted life. Lennon's emotions are like a roadmap showing me the way. It makes comprehending her feelings easy, even for a social novice like me.

She sucks in a sharp breath before stammering, "Oh m-my God. It's really you, Ryker. You're freaking huge!" Her irises expand before she slaps a hand over her gaping mouth. Red blotches her creamy skin as she continues watching me. The intensity in her aqua pools swallows me and all I can do is tread water while waiting for more. Her trembling fingers slowly move across her blushing cheek. "What did I just say? I'm such an idiot. I just . . . can't believe you're him. It's been *you* this entire time?" Her head shakes back and forth as her forehead crinkles.

I offer her a nod since my voice has slunk back into hiding.

Lennon blinks and dips her quivering chin without saying anything. She keeps her wise eyes locked on me under lowered lids. My shoes shuffle on the concrete floor as I fight against the tension in my muscles. Is she waiting for me to speak? What am I supposed to say? Does she want me to leave? My brain stalls out as anxiety fills my torso, making it difficult to breathe. My thumb rubs circles against my fingertips as nerves boil higher.

"Are you going to say anything?" Lennon blurts, saving me from a mental breakdown. I need her to take charge of this conversation.

My shoulders lift in a helpless shrug, unsure what she expects.

Does she remember anything else other than my name? Such as my nonexistent speech?

We haven't uttered a word to each other since the day my destiny was set in motion. I had so many questions back then but was riddled with uncertainty. No matter how badly my mouth urged me to utter words of want and desire, I remained silent. Lennon never tried interacting with me either, which made me believe she didn't like me. Even as a friend. What girl would approach the hulking freak that never talks?

She hums while nodding. "Still the strong and silent type, then?"

Now it's my turn to give her a wide-eye stare while a slight smile curves her mouth.

"I haven't forgotten, Ryker. But time changes people so you might have become a chatterbox." A tinkling giggle accompanies her words and I wonder if that was a joke. "Urgh, sorry. That was lame, and probably insensitive. I'm super nervous and not handling this well. I never talk to guys. Like ever. Do you know that about me? From watching me?" Her soothing tone eases the worry in my veins but the reminder of my stalking habits has my teeth grinding together.

I decide to be honest and give her another nod. But irritation prods at me for being a chicken shit. My eyes clench shut as I force out a muted, "Yes."

Her lips buzz together as she blows out a huge exhale. "I'm trying to wrap my head around . . . all of this." She's waving her arms between us and it seems like she's beckoning me forward. My feet automatically move to erase some of the distance, until she's near enough to touch if warranted. Lennon doesn't appear to mind my proximity but I don't dare get closer. Not yet.

She looks up at me with a furrow back in her brow. "Why? Tell me why you've been following me all this time."

I gulp down the sand coating my dry mouth before asking, "Are you angry?"

"That doesn't answer my question but if you're wondering, I'm more curiously befuddled. Does that make sense? I just don't get it. And I'd like to understand, Ryker. I *really* would. You saved me from something awful but never mentioned it again. You all but ignored me after that day in high school. What you did, how you stepped in to help without pause, meant so very much to me. I wanted us to be . . . friends, or at least talk sometimes. Any acknowledgement of my presence would have been nice but I got nothing." She bites her pouty lip before her eyes narrow into slits. "I know those jerks spread rumors about me but that's all they were. It was a bunch of assholes telling lies." Lennon spits the last part.

She's tossing so much at me that my brain is having difficulty settling on the appropriate reaction. She wanted me to talk to her? She was waiting for me to pay attention? Lennon clearly has no idea that she owns every single piece of me.

But what stands out the most is I know exactly what she means, and that flips something very significant within me.

We have something in common.

For the first time, I'm actually understanding what someone feels without grinding gears to figure it out. That alone lifts a burden that always sinks me down.

We were waiting for each other.

But then I remember what else she said.

Those fucking pieces of shit were picking on my sunshine. Lennon's words spread a thick layer of dense fury through me.

The mention of high school is like an angry fog that's never far from descending. Knowing she was a victim of their cruelty adds another scorching layer of hate.

I'm ready to find their locations and unleash the venom harbored against them but she jumps back in.

"So, was that it? Did you stay away from me because of their stupid stories? But then why follow me? I don't get it," she states.

"I actually know you . . . well, at least I knew who you *were*. All this time, I'd been convinced a stranger was watching me, and now, I discover it wasn't a random person at all. Why didn't you say something sooner? Why did you wait years to show yourself? Why hide from me? Why the secrets? Just . . . why?"

Lennon's eyes shine with tears as her volume raises with each question. She spins around before standing from the seat. Her fingers spear into her glossy hair as she takes a few steps toward a big window along the back wall. I watch as her back quakes with shuddering breaths. "I'm really upset, Ryker." She spells it out clear as day so even I can understand.

Yet I find myself shocked silent *again*. Revealing my deeply ingrained obsession will surely terrify her. I imagine her walking away from me and feel ill. I need to fix this without losing her but how the hell am I supposed to do that?

With Lennon facing away, I can't concentrate on anything but her shutting me out. A plea is waiting on my lips, ready to beg for her turquoise sea and sunny rays. Cold sweat prickles my skin. Everything aches as I rack my feeble brain for a plan. My heart jolts as I recall her question from this morning and settle on that. It's a way of telling her how I feel without saying too much.

With a relieved whoosh, I give her one word. "Yes."

Lennon twirls around in the next breath, sputtering and

shaking her head. "Yes to what, Ryker? That doesn't go along with anything I've been talking about."

I swallow my fear. "Yes, I like you. A lot." Those words have been suffocating me, taunting me for keeping quiet, and hopefully sharing them is the right choice.

Her eyes become saucer sized as she stumbles closer. I almost reach out to balance her when she grabs hold of the nearby table. "What did you say?" she whispers.

"You asked earlier. I mean, you asked the hooded stranger, if he liked you. If that's why he was following you. Well, he is me and yes, I like you." The explanation tumbles out—no filter or second thought.

Without warning, she leaps toward me. Every instinct within me reaches out to catch her as my arms pull her tight against me. The top of her head meets the ball of my collarbone and it's a natural fit. My chin rests on her crown as she snuggles into my chest. As a person who's never liked being touched, I should be uncomfortable with what's happening but everything I am welcomes her against me, easily and effortlessly, like finding a salve for an untreatable wound.

Just as the last of my festering unease dissipates, Lennon starts pushing away from me. I tighten my hold, nowhere near ready to let her go, as she gasps loudly, "Holy shit, what's wrong with me? I just freaking mauled you! I've never done anything like this, ever!" Her long hair whips around as she jerks back. "All of a sudden something snapped and I flung into you, like an effing rubber band. It was like an out-of-body experience, like some . . . subconscious shit I couldn't control. Does that sound totally crazy? Oh my God, you must think I'm looney." Lennon keeps struggling and puts a hand to her creased forehead. I swear this isn't normal for me. I don't go around throwing myself at guys—"

I cut her off right there. "Please, stop."

She does immediately.

"It's okay, Lennon. I'm perfectly all right with what's happening here."

Her bottomless eyes flash at me. "You are? Really?"

"Of course. I'm pretty damn crazy about you so having you here," I squeeze her gently, "means a lot."

She murmurs quietly, "I've been waiting a long time to hear that. You have no idea."

"It makes you happy I feel that way?" The answer might be obvious to some but I need her words.

"Very much. I've, Ummm . . . never forgotten about you. I had a crush on you in high school." Lennon groans before turning her face into my shirt. "I'm such a dork. Who just blurts something like that out?" Her question is muffled.

"Well, me. I just did that. Right? I like you and had a . . . crush on you back then too." What I feel is far more than a simple crush but that's the term she chose.

Lennon laughs and the sound vibrates through me.

"We're quite unique. Most people censor what they say and aren't so open. I've always held back but it's different with you. I kept my feelings secret for so long and now you're here . . . it makes sense to share it."

Her words make my body lock up tight. Lennon only knows a portion of my possessive devotion to her. I need to be perfectly typical otherwise.

Lennon pulls back and looks up at me. "What's wrong?"

Uncertainty pokes at my mind. I don't know how to describe

the thoughts quickly spinning through me. My brain is at war with my heart, pulling me in different directions. I glance away before muttering, "I don't want to be different anymore."

"What do you mean? We'll always be—"

I cut her off with a sharp, "No. I need to be normal."

Lennon noticeably flinches before pushing further away. She doesn't look at me while mumbling, "All right. That's fine. I didn't mean to offend you or anything." She laughs but there's no joy behind it, as though it's shoved from her lungs. "I don't think it's a bad thing to be different. Guess you don't feel the same way." Her tone is flat and dull, lacking the usual vibrancy.

"I don't understand. Do you want me to leave?" I manage to ask weakly.

She offers a barely-there shrug before tightly wrapping her arms around her waist. *Shit, I said the wrong thing.* She wants me to go, for real this time. Terror grips my windpipe because I just blew my only chance with her. I can't go back to the shadows. I won't survive without her warmth.

Fuck, my lungs are burning.

Black spots dance in my vision. I'm screaming on the inside, flipping my shit, yet outwardly I'm still rooted in place. *Don't take the sunshine away,* bubbles in my strangled throat but can't be voiced in the midst of panic.

"Ryker? Hey, are you alright?" Lennon is standing directly before me but not close enough to cork the erupting hysteria.

Anxiety threatens to crush me so all I can do is shake my head.

I jump when her heated palms cover my shaking fists but the gentle touch is a heated balm to my numb limbs. My crazed stare sears into her calm gaze as she brings me back from the ledge.

"I don't want you to go, Ryker. You seemed upset so I figured you wanted space. That's all." Lennon speaks quietly and her silky tone cocoons me in peace. Her nails softly scratch my forearms and the sensation dives down into my marrow.

This girl is . . . life changing.

She clears her throat. "Can we start over? Like, erase the last thirty minutes?"

Fear of rejection stabs me but I give her honesty. "Holding you in my arms was the best thing that's ever happened to me. I don't want to pretend that didn't happen. *No way.*"

Lennon smiles and bliss spreads outward from my chest. "Just the misunderstanding, not the hug. I don't want to forget that either."

I focus on her glistening lips, plump and turned up at the corners. The matching grin feels foreign on my face yet natural for her at the same time. The lingering tension disappears as I get lost in her. "So, what happens now?"

nine

LENNON

A SLIGHT SMIRK CURLS HIS mouth and the glorious sight steals my focus, along with any intention of discussing why or when he started following me. Why do we need to delve directly into the tough stuff anyway? I was already upset as the frustration of him ignoring me in school came rushing out. I couldn't control the outpouring of emotion that's been waiting directly under the surface but that's not how this long overdue reunion should have started.

I want to bask in joyful celebration.

Ryker is here.

How is this real? Would it be completely inappropriate to continue staring at him without speaking? He's my hero and has been since saving me from a horrible situation I couldn't have stopped alone. I'll never forget what Ryker did for me and hopefully my appreciation still shines brightly through the shock.

He doesn't seem to mind the quiet and from what I recall, he never did back then either. Ryker never spoke to anyone, at least from my careful observations, but I always waited for him to talk to me. Each day I sat silently in front of him believing he never noticed me. Even after he rescued me from Jason, and my infatuation morphed into an unrequited crush, we never interacted again.

I've been given a second chance.

Should I say something to break up the silence?

My brain hasn't quite caught up to my heart and keeps tripping up in disbelief. He's breathtaking and strong and . . . standing so close I can almost touch him. Ryker is effing stunning, like break-the-rating-scale type of hottie. I tip my chin further back to get the full picture—might as well since I'm already gawking like a lovestruck fangirl.

He's massive, but always was so that's not what I'm paying attention to. Ryker always hid his stunning blue eyes behind a curtain of shaggy hair. The thick dark brown thatch would hang over his face, protecting him from lingering stares. For three months I sat in front of him and always wondered what it'd be like to have his ocean gaze directly on me. Well, now I know.

Ryker is the one I've been waiting for.

The mere idea of him has been keeping me company all this time, along with my secret admirer, but of course they're one in the same. As if my point needs more proof, I'm able to talk openly to him without an ounce of fear. Even with his intense blues blazing at me, my belly flutters in glee without a twinge of anxiety. If I wasn't stuck in Lalaland, the words would flow easily like a waterfall. In this moment, I'm experiencing complete obliteration of appropriate brain functioning and social skills.

Cue the verbal vomit.

"What happened to your hair?" The urge to smack my forehead tingles my fingertips but I shake it off.

Seriously, Lennon?

Gah, I'm so awkward. Out of everything there is to ask, I choose to point out his change in appearance. Real winner, right here. Ryker doesn't catch my internal struggle and answers my ridiculous question without hesitation.

"I want you to see me."

My loopy mind screeches to a halt. "Wh-what?" I gulp down a bundle of nerves. "That's the sweetest thing anyone has ever said to me."

He nods sharply. "Good. That's how it should be. I like you and want to make you happy, so that makes sense. Right?"

I offer a soft, "Yes."

He tosses out amazing lines, full of feeling, without thinking twice. Similar to his romantic notes, these words take my breath away and leave me off kilter. I'm not sure how to handle such raw honesty, especially after Ryker told me he doesn't want to be different. This conversation is the definition of different, at least in my sliver of experience.

The way he speaks his mind without filter is a rare trait I haven't found in another person. I've always felt it was best to be open and honest to avoid misunderstanding but earlier, I managed to upset Ryker without realizing it. I figured he would be alright walking on the odd side with me, but maybe not. My need to know what bothered him pokes at me while I stare at his relaxed face. Ryker brings forward a lot of questions that muddle my already confused mind. Such as his desire to fit in and not stand out but he's been blurting out sentences without preamble. Does he realize the contradiction? Should I point it out? How am I supposed to handle this?

Obviously, I'm not an expert on acceptable flirting behavior.

According to Lucy there are rules for dating. I've never understood why girls need mind games and manipulation to land a boyfriend but she swears that type of stuff is expected. Why should I wait for him to call? What if I want to express my true feelings? Why would I pretend to be busy when he asks me out? I always cringe when she brings this up because it makes finding love seem cheap and fake. I don't want to act like a broken see-saw.

Clearly Ryker isn't typical, which makes my spirit soar. I don't want to use Lucy's dumb list either. But what should I do next? So far, he seems fairly content just standing close to me. We can't just stare silently at one another all night. That would be . . . too weird. I think?

Am I supposed to start a discussion? Ask him everything I want to know? My mind is a tangle of turmoil because I've never done this before. Threads of panic lace around my neck but I shove them away. I don't want to screw this up again but he needs to accept that I'm different. Whether he wants to be or not. I won't pretend to be someone I'm not, even for Ryker.

I chew on my lip while glancing away from his searing stare. When he grunts, my gaze refocuses on him but maybe I shouldn't have. Ryker is grinding his teeth while his nostrils flare with a huge exhale. My head tilts as I study his features.

"Is something wrong?"

Ryker's jaw works back and forth. "I've been waiting so long to stand in front of you, just like this. I've imagined it so many times over the years. I want us to talk but . . . I don't know what to say. I'm . . . frustrated about that. I don't want to be silent while I'm with you. I've spent my entire life in silence. Can you . . . please tell me what to say?" He blows out another breath and I imagine that took guts to admit. He's being brave so I should too.

I have questions, so very many that really need answers. My memory keeps circling back to Ryker ignoring me in school. Every day I waited for his ocean waves to crash into me but they never did. I clear the dryness from my throat. "Can we go back to the beginning? Like four years ago?" Ryker shrugs before nodding. An idea pops up and I blurt, "Oh! Can we also make a deal?"

"Like what?" His tone is gruff as he squints at me.

"Well, I really don't want to make you mad again—"

He interrupts. "You didn't make me mad."

"All right. Ummm . . . whatever you want to call what happened earlier. With the whole 'being different' thing." I use air quotes and heat scorches my face for being a dork. "We want us to be honest with each other, right? I don't want to tiptoe on eggshells and be afraid to speak my mind. Don't shut me out if I say the wrong thing, okay? This is all new to me."

Ryker stretches his fingers before shoving them deep into his pockets. He kicks at the floor before catching my unwavering stare again.

"Okay. I always want the truth from you, Lennon. And I'll be honest too." His chest lifts with a big sigh. "I've always been the outcast because people were scared of me but . . . the feeling was mutual. I was fine with it, until you showed up. I don't want to be different or weird in your eyes. I just want to be normal. *For you.*"

This enormous man just wants to be understood and

maybe . . . loved. His admission has emotion clouding my vision. Ryker uses his thick thumb to wipe the tear streaking down my cheek, like he did this morning. I chuckle lightly while my insides turn into gooey mush. "Oh, wow. I had no idea you even noticed me back then. Now I'm not sure what to say," I murmur as my shoulders hitch up.

He snorts. "Are you joking? You're all I think about." An adorable blush colors his face when he adds, "You're my sunshine."

I shiver when that name leaves Ryker's lush lips. His husky tone sparks some serious desire in my veins, sending another tremor through my limbs.

"Are you cold?" He asks softly.

Before I can say anything, Ryker pulls me into his arms. Even though my skin is blazing hot, I'd never complain about being close to him. My cheek rubs against comfortable worn cotton and his heart pounds steadily against my ear. A happy sigh escapes me.

I could definitely get used to this.

Ryker hums before resting his chin on my head. "Better?"

"Oh, yes. This is perfect." I nestle deeper into his embrace and let the moment swallow me up. Because I'm toasty warm with happiness wafting off me like an expensive perfume, my inhibitions loosen. "Why do you follow me?"

He's silent for a few beats before his muttered response vibrates against me. "Isn't it obvious?"

I shake my head while saying, "No. Not to me."

Ryker moves us to a nearby workstation and leans back against the table, making sure to never break our connection. We settle into the new position before he replies.

"You're not going to get upset? Run off scared or anything?" His voice holds a decent dose of fear and I want to settle his nerves.

"Of course not. I need to know why."

"The honest truth?" He pauses for a long breath. "I can't leave you alone. For my own sanity and well-being, I need to stay close. All the time. If I can't see you, my lungs seize up and panic closes in. I constantly worry something will happen to you if I'm not there. Or you'll disappear and I won't be able to find you. What started as a teenage crush has grown into much more. I'll admit that stalking you probably wasn't the best way to show my feelings but it just . . . happened. I need to protect you and keep you safe. Always. No matter what." His arms tighten around me, as if trapping me in place.

I manage to squeeze even closer on my own. "Whoa, really? Wasn't expecting that at all. But for real, it doesn't scare me. There's something about you that's always drawn me in. I just wish you wouldn't have kept it a secret."

"Yeah, I know. Me too." His words puff against my hair.

I lick my dry lips before diving in deeper. "So, why didn't you talk to me again after that shit with Jason?"

Ryker tenses and grips onto my shirt tighter. "I wanted to, Lennon. I thought about approaching you every day. My confidence wasn't great and after years of verbal lashings and vicious torment, any lingering shreds were decimated. Even though it was difficult to breathe without you around, I waited for you to approach me. Days piled on top of weeks and before I knew it, graduation arrived and my time was up. I had a lot of chances but blew them all. I settled for watching you from a distance and keeping you safe that way."

I relax against his strong build as realization strikes. I'm incredibly protected and Ryker will slay all my monsters. I just wish this connection happened sooner. "Those stupid jerks ruin everything. How did they get away with it for so long? Didn't you ever report the bullying?"

His right shoulder hitches up before he tells me, "Snitches get stitches. Besides, I handled it my own way."

"How?"

"Let's save that for a different day, yeah? Can we talk about something else?" The plea is clear in his raspy voice.

My head bobs slowly and I bite my lip, deciding what to ask next. "So, after all this time, why did you choose to finally reveal yourself? Don't get me wrong, I'm sure happy you did but was there a reason?" I inhale his addictive musk and hold back an embarrassing purr.

Ryker sighs softly. "I was tired of staying away. Each day, I became a bit more desperate to get closer. For a long time, the distance didn't seem so bad but suddenly I couldn't rest until you noticed me. Even if it was in a small way. Plus, you're about to graduate again and I didn't want to wait until it was too late. I was just . . . ready."

"That's really romantic," I whisper with whimsy coating my words.

Doesn't every girl want a boy to follow her wherever she goes?

Ryker jolts back against the table. "You think me stalking you is romantic?" Disbelief hangs thick from his tone.

I lightly swat his pec. "I don't like that word. I prefer protecting or watching."

"How are you okay with it? Me following you?"

My shoulders bunch around my ears. "I don't really know how to describe it. I guess, I like that there is someone out there who finds me special enough to seek out. All those gifts and notes over the years? I've saved and cherished each one. Who wouldn't love that kind of attention? It's not like you ever threatened me or freaked me out. You were like an invisible friend, somewhere out there for me to cling to." *Gah, I sound like a nut.* The strain in my upper body relaxes with a heavy breath. "I'd never had anyone really care for me before. My parents love me, sure, but they never gave me affection or positive attention. They pushed me to do well in school and sheltered me from any trouble. You know what I mean?"

Ryker's eyes lose focus as he mutters, "Yeah. I get it."

"Want to tell me about it?"

His gaze shifts back to me. "Nah, another time." That makes two deflections but my heart is happy with what he's shared.

My stomach suddenly growls loudly and I hunch slightly to silence the gurgle. "Urgh, sorry. It's way past dinnertime."

"Fuck, I'm an idiot." Ryker growls while shoving away from the desk. He keeps his arms around me but the mood has completely changed. "I was supposed to bring you food. It's Thursday and you always work late. It slipped my mind since I got here before picking anything up. *Shit.*" His body is rigid and practically vibrates with tension.

I dig my short nails into his strong back. "Hey, now. Don't be silly. I would much rather have you here with me." My fingers push harder until he looks down at me. "You don't have to do all that stuff for me. I'm capable of getting my own dinner, especially if it means spending more time with you."

Ryker grunts and his neck ripples with a jerky swallow. "I'm supposed to take care of you. That includes feeding you when you're hungry."

"Well, why don't we go together?"

"What do you mean?" he asks with a raised brow.

I smirk at his inquisitive expression. "Let's go to a restaurant, grab a bite, keep chatting . . . what do you say? It'll be our first date."

Ryker is already shaking his head before I finish talking. "No. That is not how our first date is supposed to go. Not a chance. Plus, crowds aren't my thing. I much prefer takeout."

He's already thought about our first date?

My lips purse as I mull that over. Ryker just gave me an idea for later but for now, I'm focusing on food—however I can get it. "What type of food should we get? If you're all right with us eating together on a first non-date." I hum at his stony features, not a grin in sight.

"I want to do everything with you. We can get whatever you want," his grumble moves through me as I think about him offering me *everything*. My cheeks flush and I bury my face against his firm chest.

Gah, I'm such a dork.

I clear my throat. "Well, aren't you Mr. Agreeable. What if I want anchovies and sardines?"

Ryker doesn't look the least bit disgusted by my suggestion. A deep rumble drops from his mouth and completely derails my thoughts, especially when those magnificent lips form beautiful words.

"Anything for you, Sunshine."

I'VE NEVER FELT LIKE THIS before.

Everything is completely weightless as I soar high above the clouds without a worry on my mind. The girl of my dreams is walking beside me, completely aware of my existence, after sharing a delicious meal together. My heart beats an ecstatic rhythm as a smile hijacks my features, showing everyone just how fucking happy I am.

Let them gawk and be jealous—I'll even keep my hood down.

My legs stretch ten feet with the pride surging through me. Does Lennon realize I noticed the subtle moves she was making earlier? Like sniffing my shirt or rubbing her cheek against my pec or slowly walking her fingers up my ribcage? If she's trying to be sneaky or stealthy, it's definitely not working. I'm completely blown away and totally perplexed that she's chosen me but . . . these seemingly small tricks are driving me crazy with want. I don't know how to handle the lust sprouting and growing like a wild ivy inside of me. Is she doing this on purpose? Trying to get me riled up with desire?

The idea makes me float even higher into the atmosphere, where nothing bad can ever harm me again. Lennon, my beautiful sunshine, wants to be near me. More than that, she *likes* me—stalker parts and all.

This is going to work out between us . . .

"What put that adorable smile on your face?" Her honey voice drips with sugary sweetness as we stroll along the path toward home.

Maybe I should feel emasculated that the term *adorable* is used to describe anything about me but Lennon can say whatever the hell she wants. I'll consider myself lucky that she even talks to me.

I glance at her and find those gorgeous aqua eyes already looking my way. "You. Always you."

Lennon giggles. "Ryker, you're spoiling me. How'd you get to be so romantic?"

You is the word once again sticking to my tongue but I decide to be more creative. "I have the greatest inspiration and you're meant to be treated like a queen."

"Well, you're doing a heck of a job already. I'm like a giddy pre-teen going gaga over her first as they hold hands. Like, *omggggg!*" When Lennon squeals, I almost laugh but then she groans and covers her blushing face.

I twist toward her. "What's wrong? Why is your face all red?"

"Urgh, because I'm embarrassed. Who says stuff like that?

Why am I so weird?" She whines and I want to wrap her in a hug.

"I really like the random stuff that pops out of your mouth. Although it'd be hard to find anything I don't enjoy about you."

Lennon huffs lightly. "See? You're way too biased. Anyone else would think I'm a loon."

"Good thing no one else matters then."

She stares up at me, her light eyes shining, like she's got a special secret. "No one else matters," she echoes.

We arrive at the apartment complex and my chest contracts at the thought of saying goodnight. My muscles convulse with dread as my brain scrambles for something to say.

Lennon steals the words from me. "Today has been unexpectedly wonderful. I had no idea that you'd be here, standing in front of me. I wouldn't have ever hoped for that." She takes a deep breath while narrowing the small gap between us. "Thank you for everything, Ryker. For helping me back then and for coming back to me now. You're everything I've dreamed of and hopefully we'll be spending a lot more time together."

I drag her tiny frame into my bulk. My voice is a murmur against her dark hair, "I'm the one who's thankful. I never thought you'd accept me with such open arms. This couldn't have gone better, even in my wildest fantasies."

Lennon purrs, "Fantasies? That sounds interesting."

My face flames as tension locks up my body. My taut control almost snaps from the exaggerated force stretching in two directions. The dirty cravings for Lennon's body have been getting more powerful, practically interrupting my every thought. Yet, this newly uncovered bond between our hearts is still fragile and I'm not about to destroy my chances.

Her melodic laugh breaks the pressure pounding through me,

especially when she whispers, "Just kidding. You looked totally freaked out for a second there."

A weighty exhale deflates my chest and Lennon nuzzles closer. I'm more than happy to let *that* subject drop—for now.

"So, I'll walk you to class tomorrow morning. Unless you'd prefer I keep my distance like usual. It's up to you but making sure you're safe isn't negotiable."

"No more hiding, Ryker. I want you to be with me, not following behind. The new usual is right next to me, okay?" Lennon leaves no room for argument, not that I would.

I nod in easy agreement, relishing in the sunny warmth beaming into my bloodstream. My hands grip her hips, reluctant to let her go, but knowing she needs sleep. "I'll see you in the morning, Sunshine."

Lennon's fingers clasp onto my shirt and dig in as she tilts her head up. "I don't want you to leave. How far away do you live? Who's going to protect you?" She asks with a tremble in her pouty lip. Her worry for me is heavenly but totally unnecessary. My spirit skyrockets with the fact that she cares about me.

"Nah, my place is real close. I'll be just fine. Sweet dreams, yeah?" My scruffy cheek rests on her smooth forehead. The urge to kiss her soft skin rams into me but I don't want to ruin this moment with a wrong move.

She sighs and pulls away, taking her blanket of warmth with her.

"My dreams are always sweet because the beautiful blue ocean and crashing waves keep me company. I hope you sleep well too. Thanks again . . . for everything."

I'm not sure what she means but it sounds nice. A small grin lifts one side of her mouth as she gives a tiny wave before walking up the steps. I watch her heavenly curves dip and sway as desperation to follow claws at me. Somehow, I resist the temptation and watch her retreating form disappearing from sight.

I yank my hood up and trudge off toward Mac's, a gym across the street. The comfort Lennon provided me is enough to replace the typical bang of aggression but there's still an edge of restlessness in my system. I'd rather cozy up against the wall shared with Lennon's apartment but working out my excess energy is part of my routine. I can't be getting soft and start slacking off. Pushing myself to exhaustion will help me focus on the work I have to do later.

My mind switches to autopilot as I stomp down the rickety stairs into the underground. As I walk into the dank lobby, the owner lifts his chin in greeting. Words aren't necessary here, that's what sold me on this place. The concrete floor is stained with sweat and the chipped walls are crumbling so I fit right in. Outer appearances mean shit.

In the years I've been coming here, no one ever interferes or interrupts. It's an unspoken agreement and everyone is expected to sign on the invisible line. We're here to blow off steam, not make friends. If I ever need a spotter, someone will silently help out but we never exchange more than a wave or salute. That's more than enough communication for me.

I toss my sweatshirt into a dusty corner as I warm up on an ancient treadmill, ignoring the rust and grime. My thoughts drift away as my rapid heart rate pounds like a stampede of wild horses. Perspiration drips from my temple and the toxic voices seep out with each drop. I'm not a creep or freak and my eyes aren't crazy. Lennon never talks to guys but she's chosen me to spend time with. That's all I need in this fucked up world.

Each push and pull, strain and shove, is for her. I force myself faster and harder, picturing her smiling face at the finish line. Tendrils of lust claw into my torso and I pump the weights at lightning speed to stave off the increasing desire. I need to be stronger, faster, and more powerful to ensure my body is an unstoppable machine against potential threats. I can't stop until my mind is quiet. One-hour bleeds into two and my entire body aches from the grueling circuit. The nonstop assault on my muscles ensures every piece of me is worn the fuck out.

My sluggish feet stumble home far past midnight. I've still got a lot of work ahead of me but this is the money-making kind. As my numb legs give out, I collapse into the desk chair and listen for any sign of Lennon being awake. She never is but that doesn't stop my starving ears from straining to hear the lovely notes of her voice.

I crack open my laptop before rolling my stiff neck, prepping for the pile of shit before me. Ignoring the corporate clowns and their demanding emails isn't hard but the cash flow will run dry if I don't comply eventually. They've been getting antsy without the daily security protection report, not that they truly understand the laundry list of numbers and figures I send out.

Such is my life after dark.

My screen floods with black and green as my fingers and mind work in tandem to scour the encryption code for any leaks. Once I'm assured the software is flawless and running as usual, I begin checking the company databases for breaches. This process has become second-nature and doesn't take much effort anymore. Other than Lennon, hacking is all I know and years have been dedicated to shaping these skills into something relatively good.

A breach alert interrupts my steady flow, warning me that

someone's trying to crack through my system's backdoor. Stupid idiot. No one can make a dent in my personalized encryption code but nice fucking try. When I see the username blasting between the streaming lines, a snort rolls from my exhausted throat.

AATS: You're a fucking tool. Stop messing around.

Dx8MM: Where the fuck you been? No one else gets my humor like you.

AATS: Miss me? No one likes it when you bust into their shit and you're slowing me down.

Dx8MM: It's all in good fun. Where you been? With the girl?

AATS: Yup.

Dx8MM: Fuck that. That's all I get after helping you?

I suppose he deserves a few crumbs after listening to my random rants about Lennon after all this time.

AATS: We talked today. And I'm walking her to class tomorrow. She knows about the stalking.

Dx8MM: And the personalized security detail?

AATS: Not exactly.

Dx8MM: You're screwed.

An email notification pops up and distracts me from the bullshit with D. I switch screens and scan the message quickly.

It's a response to my inquiry about a rental property Lennon had bookmarked last week. Denten is a cozy area nestled far off the beaten city path. I've known Lennon has had her eye on moving to a small town for a while and that suits me just fine. The fewer people, the fucking better. I'd happily move to the middle of nowhere with just my girl in tow.

The building space will be vacant on the first of July, which is less than two months away. Lennon has access to the studio on campus through the summer but perhaps she'd skip out of this crowded college hotspot early if it meant having her dream location. This property is perfect for a workroom or a fully functioning store, depending on what Lennon wants. As of now, she's doing all her sales online but that could change. It's always nice to have the flexibility and options.

Why wouldn't she agree?

I'm sure she'll go for it . . . once she realizes this is a possibility. I just have to figure out how to set it up so she doesn't see out how deep my involvement runs. At least not until I'm certain she won't leave me. I need her to love me, truly and unconditionally, before the entire truth comes out. In the meantime, I'll work even harder at becoming the man Lennon wants to spend her life with. A guy lucky enough to deserve all of her.

I wrap up the InfoSec reports and send them off with a heavy sigh, glad to be done with the repetitive routine. The darkest parts of my night are always the same without Lennon. I've never been a strong sleeper but at this point, my chaotic mind is ready to shut down like the computer before me. My head bobs and my eyelids feel like sandbags. As my mind starts drifting, images of a white picket fence and a quaint yellow home flicker in my subconscious before the darkness engulfs me.

eleven

LENNON

I haven't visited the ocean or swam in the sea. I've been too busy drowning in his crystal-clear depths.

THE EARLY MORNING SUN IS already shining bright when I step outside. The Michigan climate easily slides from spring to summer this time of year and I welcome the humidity after months of dry static. Green grass decorates the ground in neon patches while pink blossoms bud on the trees. A breeze spreads the smell of fresh flowers into the air and my lungs greedily suck in the sweet scent. The lush scenery isn't what I'm really interested in though.

After a few beats with my face tilted toward the warm rays, I lower my gaze, ready to find Ryker. I find him standing directly in front of me, leaning against a stone pillar with his hands full of my favorite breakfast goodies. My heart melts at his thoughtfulness as my stomach gurgles happily. Ryker straightens before moving closer, keeping his sights on me as a slight grin curls his tempting lips.

I wave and a blush creeps up my neck, unsure what to do while his scorching stare blasts straight to my core. Suddenly the balmy weather isn't what's heating me up. Just as I'm about to greet him properly, Lucy busts through the front door behind me.

"Urgh, sorry. My mom called and wanted to chat about this weekend. She should know this is the worst time to call." She huffs and stops beside me.

My neck twists to her before turning back to Ryker. The joy drops from his mouth as he stares wide-eyed in our direction. He's frozen solid but the cup and bag in his hands tremble. His gaze darts around wildly, as if looking for an escape out of this sticky situation. My chest cramps painfully at the clear discomfort marring his features and I'm eager to soothe his worry.

"Holy shit." Lucy whistles quietly.

I shoot her a death glare—*do not embarrass me.*

She either doesn't get the memo or chooses to ignore it.

"So, this is the infamous Seek? I suppose the appeal is clear," Lucy mutters while scanning Ryker's motionless form. I recognize the flare of interest in her brown gaze and bitter jealousy rears its head. I'm about to growl all sort of obscenities when her eyes dart back to me. "All right, I totally get it." A short burst of laughter tumbles out.

I shake my head, completely confused. "Huh?"

"I'd let that sexy Manwich follow me around too." Lucy nods toward Ryker.

My eyes shift back to him and my tears threaten at his ghostly appearance. "Are you being serious right now?" I bite out between clenched teeth.

Her forehead creases as she shrugs. "Ummm, yeah. I'm supporting your coocoo case. Figured you'd be happy about that."

"I don't need your approval." I scoff while bumping into her.

"Pretty sure you do. That guy," she gestures blindly to Ryker, "is crazy about you. That look he's got? You're his stars, moon, and sun above. Pretty sure this is way above your head, Lenny, but I'll help." Lucy's voice is gentle as she lightly touches my arm. I barely notice since my concentration is solely focused on Ryker's gorgeous face.

My sunshine.

Lucy makes a strange noise so I quickly glance at her. "Just as I suspected. You look at him the exact same way."

"I do?" Not sure the question is needed since that's exactly how I feel. Having her confirmation makes the possibility of love an absolute reality that's sinking deep into me.

Her hand gently squeezes me.

"Why are you still standing here with me? Shouldn't you go over there or something? Pretty sure he's not getting closer."

I'm trapped by his stormy-sky eyes and a ball of desperation grows in my chest. Stupid me, I should already be wrapped around him, reassuring him that everything's all right.

"Go get your guy," Lucy murmurs before giving me a little shove. Before I can say anything else, she hops down the stairs and strolls off toward campus.

I bite my lip while trying to swallow the fizzing nerves suddenly rising in my throat. There's no reason for worry but Lucy's words have slipped a new awareness into my inexperienced brain. What I share with Ryker is *serious*.

My steps are slow as I approach him, never taking my eyes off his somber expression. Worry lines are etched around his tense features and purple smudges sit under his ocean eyes. When I stop in front of him, my body automatically sways closer as his magnetic aura draws me in. His rich woodsy essence surrounds me and I resist the urge to rub against him.

"Hi you," I whisper while nudging his foot.

Ryker clears his throat while glancing away. "Hey, Lennon. Don't you wanna walk with Lucy?"

I jolt slightly at his desolate tone. "I want to walk with you, like we planned. Is that all right?"

His light eyes flash to mine before darting away again.

"That's what I want," he mutters as his shoulders slump. The shift jostles the paper bag in his hand.

"Is that for me?"

Color returns to Ryker's face as a vibrant blush explodes. He holds the coffee and bagel higher and I eagerly take them. As my fingers wrap around the cup, I notice the yellow note attached to the side.

I peek at him from under my lashes before reading his message.

Emotion stings my eyes and I blink quickly to keep tears from falling. A soft sniffle escapes me, despite my best efforts.

"Lennon? Are you upset with me?" The crack in his voice

squeezes my heart painfully.

I wildly shake my head and step into his rigid form, trapping the treasured gifts between us.

"No. Never. You're so impossibly sweet and making me so happy."

My neck clenches with the weepy wail. Ryker loops his arms around my waist while setting his cheek against my crown, forming a protective cocoon around me.

"Why are you crying?" His deep timbre weaves into me.

"I don't know," I blubber. "You're here, waiting for me. Then you looked so distraught when Lucy showed up. I've been on such a high and seeing you upset tore me up. Then, your note with the breakfast. You're so perfect."

My tears are flowing in earnest now, soaking into his cotton shirt. My belly flutters when Ryker rubs a soothing hand up and down my back. My face heats as I attempt to snuggle closer without smashing the coffee cup.

Ryker hums before murmuring, "I'm far from perfect."

I try reining in the emotion pouring out and suck in several hearty breaths.

"We'll work on you accepting compliments," I say while blowing out a heavy sigh. "Can I ask why Lucy's presence bothered you so much? Everything seemed all right until she walked out the door. You've been near her before . . . well, before I found out who you were."

He shrugs against me before his body deflates from a heavy exhale.

"I guess she was a harsh reminder," Ryker starts slowly. "I'm alone but you have other people in your life. I forgot that it isn't just us."

I tilt my head to look at him and my chest tightens at the hollowness shining in his eyes. There's so much sadness radiating off him.

"What about your parents?"

Ryker scoffs as his gaze drifts away.

"They couldn't wait to get rid of me. We never spoke to each other, even when I was young. They always considered me a nuisance, an unsolvable problem. Not that they tried very hard." His hold around me strengthens as he grumbles through clenched teeth. "I never told them I was leaving but they'd never bother looking anyway."

Burning anger blasts through my veins at the mention of such neglect. I can't imagine what he's been through. I gulp the fury down before straightening my spine.

"Well, you have me." My tone echoes the certainty flowing through me.

"Do I really?" His question seizes my pulse.

I nod while wiggling away to set the stuff in my hands down. When I stand and face him again, our fingers lace together and rest between us. My light eyes laser into his. "Of course. Ryker, never doubt that. Don't you remember yesterday?"

"I never forget anything you say. Each moment is a cherished memory." His lush lips brush my forehead as he squeezes our palms together.

My knees wobble as the swoon-factor slams into me and my gut cues the swarming butterflies. "That right there? Wow. You know just what to say and most certainly have me. And the only other person I have is Lucy . . . and my parents, I guess. They don't really count though because I keep my distance or they'll suck me back in." I cringe, feeling guilty for pushing away their smothering love. "In a few weeks, Lucy is leaving for the entire summer so it will just be us . . . all alone. If you want me gone, you'll have to fight me off."

Ryker yanks me impossibly closer.

"That will never happen. I will always want you." The growl in his voice has tendrils of desire spreading through me and I almost choke from the sudden onslaught.

I manage to force my swollen tongue to function.

"Good. Problem solved then. Wanna sit down while I eat before walking me to class?" I gesture to a nearby bench along the sidewalk.

He nods before scooping up my breakfast and leads us down the path, managing to keep my left hand connected to his right.

"Who's Seek?" Ryker asks as he lowers down on the creaky wood.

I stumble onto the seat as my cheeks blaze.

"Um, you." I dip my chin and turn away slightly while muttering, "That was the name I came up with before I knew who you were." My eyes slam shut as embarrassment washes over me. Why couldn't Lucy keep her big mouth shut?

"You gave me a nickname?" His octave rises above his typical baritone. From the corner of my eye, I notice his face turning red too.

I bite my lip and twist back toward him.

"Yeah, but it seems silly now. Seek popped in my head one day while I was searching for you, like the game. You hide in the background and I seek you out." My jerky hands unwrap the bagel as a distraction from my rambling thoughts. I take a massive bite and immediately regret it when my eyes lift to his potent stare.

"Didn't know we were playing that. Not sure I've ever done

that before. Was I good at it?" His gaze flares with something I can't distinguish.

I nod with a mouth full of bagel before reaching for my coffee. The liquid is luke-warm but still tastes delicious as it hits my tongue. Ryker's thumb swipes at the corner of my mouth, cleaning me up, then he sucks the dab of cream cheese off his finger. My blood pressure spikes as my startled gaze spears into him. My brain activity screeches to a halt and sticks onto one central thought.

I want to know what he tastes like.

Time for my idea.

I clear my throat before diving in.

"Speaking of firsts, Ryker." I take a deep breath for courage. "I haven't done a lot of cool stuff because my parents kept me very sheltered growing up. Everyday has been the same, over and over, like I'm stuck on the carousel. Go to class, work in the studio, eat at the cafe, watch the same shows at home, then go to bed only to wake up and repeat. The routine is stale and can be recited in my sleep, like that movie *Groundhog Day*." My shoulders lift as I chuckle lightly. "There's so much out there that I've been meaning to discover. Some of the stuff is random and some is everyday type things. Like bowling. Who hasn't done that by twenty-two?"

Ryker offers a sheepish shrug and my gut confirms, once again, he's the one I've been waiting for. I reach for his hand resting on the bench between us.

"Exactly. You and me. So, I want to experience everything for the first time . . . *with you*."

His gulp is audible.

"I want that too. So much." Ryker's hoarse rasp scrapes along my heated skin.

"Great," I murmur into the shrinking space between us. "I'm glad we're on the same page. Should we start tonight? With an official first date? I've never had one."

He nods robotically as he glances between my eyes and mouth. My heartbeat booms in my ears as the possibility of rejection screams at me. The decision has already been made.

Fuck it.

When my lips lightly brush along his, Ryker startles with a gasp. I pull away and assess his wide eyes wildly scanning my face.

"What's wrong?" I whisper after backing up even further.

Color paints his cheeks as he averts his gaze.

"I've never been kissed," he mutters while glancing at me from under his long lashes.

"Me either. That was a little peck to get us started. You'll get a proper kiss later, after our date." I smile at his shy expression as excitement prickles my scalp.

Everything changes, starting today.

twelve
RYKER

LENNON KISSED ME.

It wasn't a dream when her lips briefly dusted mine but rather, an undeniable fact. That slight connection, a quick peck, over before it began, was groundbreaking. My soul wept in relief and my mind switched to slow-motion so that mere moment was playing for hours. My eyelids flutter with the memory, like watching a looped snapshot. That flicker in time is something I'll never forget.

My radiant sunshine gave her first kiss to me, a weirdo no one spares a minute for except to ridicule. Lennon is different, she always has been, she sees me, just like I always wished she would. Someone is finally giving me a chance and I'm so fucking grateful that person is her.

Our life together is finally starting. We're going on a date in less than an hour, another first for us. I'm picking her up, like a gentleman, despite her living next door. Lennon doesn't know we're neighbors yet but I'll reveal that offense tonight. Can I blame it on a strange coincidence?

Lennon seems to accept my need to keep her safe so my stomach shouldn't be in a jumble of knots. Her patience and understanding never ceases to amaze me so there's hope she'll forgive my violations of her privacy. She deserves the truth but terror scratches my skin whenever I consider exposing my secrets. I shove the mounting worry to the back of my brain and concentrate on the evening ahead.

While she's been in class, I've been busy planning a romantic outing. Too bad I don't know the first fucking thing about wining and dining the girl of my dreams. Thankfully the internet is good for more than just making money. After some research, I selected the best spot for a quiet and secluded dinner. The reviews claim the intimate Italian restaurant has the best cheesy pasta, which Lennon will appreciate it. There's a spectacular view of Lake Michigan too.

Choosing the correct flowers was another task I wasn't prepared for. After much internal debate, I settled on a bouquet of brightly blooming peonies that remind me of her vibrant aquamarine eyes. The fancy sewing machine from Lennon's wish list sits in the entryway, wrapped in pink paper and ready for her talented hands. The message boards warned me that I was going overboard but what the hell do they know? This will make her happy and I want that blinding smile aimed directly at me.

I blow out a slow breath to cool the incessant nerves poking at me. I step in front of the mirror for a final appraisal of my appearance. I've never put much thought into what clothes I'm wearing but for Lennon, I stepped out of my usual black attire. The navy and gray button-down offsets the color of my light eyes. I peer closer as the blue hues of my irises swirl together like a tragic storm.

What does she see in me?

My head jerks out of habit, expecting hair to cover the direct view. With my crazy stare still on display, I clench my lids shut and turn away. Lennon will make me feel better and I don't want to waste another moment here alone.

I grab her gifts before locking up and walking the short distance to her place. Apprehension slithers under my skin but I shake it away. Everything about tonight will be perfect, just like the woman waiting for me behind the door. I lean the heavy box against the wall before knocking hesitantly. While waiting, I hide the flowers behind my back and send off a silent wish to whoever's listening.

Please stop me from fucking this up.

With a whoosh, Lennon stands before me with an odd look crossing her glowing features. "Hey, Ryker. How'd you get in? I didn't buzz you."

She looks stunning with her long brown hair loose around her bare shoulders. Her face has a light layer of makeup that adds glitter to her skin and those lips that touched mine earlier look glossy. Lennon is still wearing the bright yellow sundress from earlier, which hints at her curves without giving too much away. When I'm done perusing her beauty, her question bangs into my distracted brain.

Shit, here goes nothing.

I gaze into her warm aqua pools and whisper another truth, "You don't have to because . . . I live in the building. Just down the hall, in 303." My head motions in the direction of my apartment.

She looks at me with a blank expression, as if her gears are grinding. Lennon's mouth is all that moves when she asks, "For real? Like, no joke?"

I shrug and bob my chin, feeling my cheeks flame.

"Huh, interesting. Do you live there on purpose? To be near me?" She tilts her head and pops out her hip.

"Yeah. That probably freaks you out, but I just want to keep you safe. To do that best, I need to be close." My voice is steady but my insides are thrashing.

Lennon hums, "Hmmm, do you like, spy on us in the shower or anything?"

"No! I would never do that," I sputter as my face tingles with shame. I've imagined watching her that way countless times, but I'd never act on those impulses.

"I'm totally messing with you," she giggles softly. The noise soothes the ragged tension in my muscles. "I'm mostly surprised you stayed out of sight this long. Lucy and I always wondered who lives there. We figured it was an older couple who never leaves."

"You're not upset?" Awe rings clear in my voice.

Lennon straightens and places her fingers around my forearm. "It doesn't bother me that you're always here if I need you, especially now that I know who you are. I think it's sweet that you watch out for me, like you can't help it. Am I romanticizing? Probably. Do I care? No." She adds pressure to her hold on me and I almost groan from the tingles zipping up my arm. "All I know is there's something special between us and we're finally going to explore it. Starting tonight, right?" My nod mirrors hers.

"Good, I'm glad we got that out of the way. Anything else you wanna share?"

My limbs lock up like concrete as my pulse roars. There's so much I need to tell her, that she deserves to know, but I can't force the words out. My eyes shift around, searching for something to anchor me. I swallow before trying again but right versus wrong keep warring in my chest.

Her candy-coated tone yanks my stare back to her. "It's alright, Ryker. You'll tell me when the time is right. Just don't hold back forever because I wanna know everything about you." Lennon points to the bouquet peeking out from behind me. "Now, those can't possibly be for me. Are you making another stop to deliver those somewhere?"

I manage to respond, "Of course they're for you. As if I'd bring gifts to anyone else." My eyes roll as I scoff. "Glad you saw them because I almost forgot."

"They're kind of hard to miss. You really shouldn't have brought me anything else. There's so much you've already done," Lennon states smoothly.

Her eyes widen when I grab the large package from the floor. "This is for you too," I explain while holding it up for her to see.

She shakes her head as the smile on her lips stretches wider. "Do you want to come in quick while I open that and get the flowers into some water?"

I nod silently before following her inside. Lennon sets the flowers on her kitchen table and I place the box down next to the blooming bundle. She motions over her shoulder. "Would you mind grabbing a vase above the sink? I always have to drag a chair over since I'm vertically challenged." She laughs while I move toward the cabinet. "I can't believe you brought me more gifts. Seriously, you're—holy shit!"

I spin around at the alarm in her voice. Lennon rips off more wrapping paper so the sewing machine image and brand name are exposed. Her trembling fingers stroke over the cardboard and my skin tightens with longing.

Great. I'm jealous of a box.

"Ryker! You bought me a *Brother SE1800*? I repeat, holy shit! This sucker costs over a thousand bucks!" Lennon's pitch is loud with excitement and a tiny grin curls my lips. Her reaction is worth every penny. I'd spend far more and expect nothing in return but her smile. The fact she's here with me, beaming so bright, is better than winning the lottery.

She lifts her shocked orbs and blasts me with overpowering light. I'll never be cold or dark again. "Ryker, I can't possibly accept this. You spent way too much money. This machine is truly amazing but I wouldn't feel right letting you pay for it."

I immediately shake my head before shutting her down. "No way. This is a gift and I want you to have it. For your own studio someday."

In the next breath, Lennon rushes over and flings her arms around me. "Thank you so much. I don't deserve all of this but please know I'm grateful. This is the sewing machine I've been saving for. How did you know?" She utters sweetly with her face tipped up to mine. There's something secret in her eyes I don't understand, or can't give so much hope to.

"You have a public wish list online. I didn't have to use any special skills to discover you wanted this." I whisper along her temple, fighting against temptation to taste her soft skin.

Her fingers dig into my sides and my control wanes when she gives a breathy sigh.

"I don't know how but everything you do is what I've always wanted. I can't wait to start our adventures."

My hands roam down her back. "Should we go? I made reservations."

Lennon nods before her eyes widen.

"Oh! I almost forgot. I have something for you."

"Lennon, you don't have to get me anything. All I want is you." I clutch her closer as my muscles constrict.

"That's not fair and don't be silly," she says and swats my chest. "I'll be right back."

Lennon dashes down a hallway as my mind whirls with wonder. What could she possibly have for me? There's nothing that could make me love her more, or so I thought.

She bounces back into the room with her hands behind her. A wide grin stretches her lips while she struts toward me. Lennon stops a foot away before rocking back on her heels.

"Don't get too excited, okay? It's nothing super special or anything. I had extra time in my seminar and was thinking of you so . . . yeah." Red creeps up her neck onto her face as she dips her chin. Lennon's left arm comes forward and I see something brown nestled in the palm.

I lean closer and realize it's . . ."A bracelet?"

Lennon nods quickly and dimples dent her blushing cheeks. "Yeah! The leather is really soft but I styled it to be masculine, just a cuff and buckle. No sparkle or fluff," she explains while unclasping the silver cinch.

My brain is jammed and I don't know what to say. All I can do is stare at the custom piece she made *for me*, and try to determine how this is real.

She makes a strange noise. "So, you hate it. Um, that's okay.

I should have known accessories weren't your thing, seeing as you don't wear any. Seriously, it was a spur of the moment—"

"I love it, Lennon," I interrupt. "No one has ever made me anything. And to be honest, I haven't received a present since grade school. Can you put it on for me?" I extend my arm after unbuttoning the shirt sleeve.

Lennon's nails scrape lightly along my skin as she attaches the cool leather around my wrist. It's like a part of her sunshine will always be with me, no matter what. I grit my teeth but a muted groan slips out. Everything this girl does drives me wild and my desire is shoving against the final strands of my resistance.

"Perfect fit," she whispers while glancing up from under hooded lids.

I fixate on the bracelet momentarily but Lennon's fingers lingering on my arm snag my focus. I'm ready for more, and hopefully she is too. My feet shuffle forward until there's mere inches between us. My chest rises and falls with my rapid breathing, suddenly nervous as fuck. My tongue sweeps along my bottom lip, erasing any dryness. I watch Lennon track the movement and that's my cue she's with me.

My palm frames her gorgeous face before tilting her jaw up toward me. Her eyes slide shut as I lower my mouth to hers, puffs of air filling the sliver of space between us. "You're so beautiful," I murmur softly before pressing our lips together.

With the initial contact, we both freeze for a single heartbeat then melt into each other. My other hand rests along her hip and hers lace around my middle. At first, I'm afraid to move as uncertainty prickles up my spine. My mouth gently settles over her glossy pout without seeking more but easily slides along the slickness. When Lennon pulls me closer, I squeeze her tighter in response and everything changes. Like a lock clicking into place, my mind catches up to my body and I figure out what happens next.

I glide my tongue along her strawberry-flavored bottom lip, like I did to my own moments before. Lennon gasps and opens for me, granting access to her sweet mouth. The first few sweeps are a burst of exotic spice after eating bland mush my entire life. I shift slightly and seal us together in a heated embrace as my lips skate along hers.

Our movements are slow but fluid, like we've been kissing for years. I softly drag her lip into my mouth while her tongue follows along, tracing my movements. Lennon gives and I take, control swapping back and forth easily. I dive into her sugary flavor before she pushes back into me for more. This kiss is like a practiced dance we never took lessons for. When Lennon scratches down my back I groan into her. Then my teeth nip lightly along her tart lips before sucking on her tongue. She moans in response and my jeans tighten uncomfortably. Our mouths keep sliding together and my eyes cross from the extreme pleasure crackling through me. Eventually my dick screams loud enough to break the spell and I realize this needs to stop before we move too fast.

When we pull apart, Lennon's face is flushed and I'm sure mine matches.

"Wow. That was really hot." She whispers against my stubbled cheek before pecking along my coarse skin. "I can't wait to do that again."

"Me too, Sunshine. You have no idea." I pant while trying to rein in my blinding lust. "I want to take you out though, like we planned." Everything below my belt begs me to reconsider when she sighs faintly.

"I suppose you're right, but that was a great way to start." She lifts a haughty brow that has me leaning closer again. "Thanks for giving me dessert first."

thirteen

LENNON

WE SETTLE INTO OPPOSITE SIDES of the darkened booth as the hostess reviews the evening's specials. I've always wanted to eat at Mustavoe's but never had the chance. This place definitely counts as an item on my 'must-experience' list. As a person who loves carbs, especially pasta, this quaint Italian spot calls to my taste buds.

"Should we get some wine?" Ryker asks after a quick glimpse at the beverage list.

I purse my lips while deciding. "Absolutely. It seems fitting for the occasion, right?" My curious gaze lands on the enormous bar that makes up the center of the restaurant.

"Alcohol will help my nerves, that's for sure."

"Nervous? With me?"

Even in the dim lighting, I see his blush. Why is that reaction so hot? Probably because Ryker is a huge presence that most wouldn't dare assume got embarrassed. The shy expression makes him even more attractive.

"There's always far too much running around up here." He taps his temple.

"Like what?" My voice rises as I lean closer.

Ryker lazily blinks several times before the openness in his eyes snuffs out. "That stuff doesn't matter now. All I care about is you having the best time tonight."

My lips purse as I let the question drop. I know he's hiding a lot under his defensive armor but there isn't much that would keep me away at this point. Ryker has occupied my fantasies for years and now that he's here, directly in front of me, it would be impossible to let go. How bad can his secrets possibly be? What could be worse than stalking?

I shake my head to wipe away those problematic thoughts, ready to enjoy the night rather than obsess over unknown possibilities. My eyes hungrily scour the extensive list of savory dishes before I sneak a quick peek at my date.

The recently introduced butterflies attack my belly as everything else fades away except this glorious front row seat to him. I stare at him unabashedly as his eyes scan the menu, completely unaware of my spying. He dressed up tonight and the effort he put into looking effing scrumptious really shows. The dress shirt stretches over his broad form every place it counts—his biceps, shoulders, and chest. My fingers fidget at the memory of the soft material covering his solid muscles and the temperature in the room suddenly spikes twenty degrees.

I blow out a long breath to cool my racing jets and lift my gaze to his other sexy features. Ryker's thick eyebrows are two dark slashes against his lightly tanned complexion. His lashes shift slightly while he reads and I'm envious of their natural volume—cursing the injustice for womankind. The unfairness scale is easily tipped the longer I look at their heart-stopping impact against the ice-blue of his eyes. Even with his handsome face slightly downcast, I can make out the high cheekbones and square jawline that pack a powerful punch to my awakening libido. Ryker's stubble is such a turn-on, especially when pressed against my delicate skin. Even though I'm burning up, a shiver wracks my limbs at the thought.

I save his mouth for last for very good reason. I have to bite my tongue when remembering his lips gliding over mine not too long ago. I glance up and my cheeks burn as Ryker's crystal eyes lock on me. Those light blue flames are throwing sparks my way, and I like to think he's recalling our kitchen kiss too. I could have spent the night wrapped in his arms while passionately connecting in that intimate way. My hips squirm on the vinyl seats as Ryker continues blasting me with blatant desire.

Holy crap, we need to talk about something before I combust.

I take a healthy sip of cool white wine to douse the lust flashing through me.

"Do you know what you're having?" I ask.

"I heard the lasagna is really good. I mean, there were a lot of great reviews for everything but that stuck out for me. What about you?"

"I'm a sucker for Mac and Cheese so that was an easy choice," I explain while closing my menu.

Ryker follows suit and the server pops over to take our order after placing a breadbasket on the table. I take a toasted slice and decide to bring up my exciting news, although the unknown details cause worry to prod at me.

"Something interesting happened to me today. I'm not sure what it means yet but it's a pretty big deal. I got an email responding to my interest in a rental property in Denten. I don't even remember filling anything out for that space because it was way out of my price range. I replied to let them know there was a mistake but it turns out, the form was definitely completed because my name and information was all correct. I've been so crazy with graduation prep and finals that it must have slipped my mind. Or maybe Lucy filled it out." A breezy laugh bubbles out of me just thinking about the stunning spot becoming mine.

Ryker stops chewing and his eyes widen as he swallows carefully. I wait for him to reply but he keeps watching me without a word.

Alrighty then.

"So, I decided to call them and it turns out the rent is far cheaper than I thought," I continue steadily. "I can't believe it. The studio is huge with a loft above so that's like a two-for-one. Plus, that little town is adorable. This seems like fate pulling strings. First, you step out of the shadows and give me everything I've wanted from a relationship. Now, I have this perfect location to start my career. I'm over the freaking moon!" I clap excitedly as a huge grin takes over my face.

When Ryker still doesn't say anything, my giddiness deflates.

"I don't have to decide right away. The lease wouldn't start until July and they're willing to hold the spot until the start of June. I let them know we'd have to discuss it." I reach for his hand and lace our fingers together. "I want you to come with me, if you're willing. I think you'd love the area. It's a cute little town with plenty of open space. Maybe we can go look at the place?" My plea is clear and hopefully he hears it. This is something I want us to experience together.

Ryker seems to gather his bearings as he squeezes my palm and shoots me a tiny grin. "That's amazing news, Lennon. I'm happy that you're happy. That's all I want. I can't wait to hear more about it."

"What's wrong, Ryker? You got all quiet and stock-still. What just happened there?" I question with a raised brow.

He scrubs his free hand down his strained face while blowing out a heavy breath. "Fuck, I'm sorry. Having these discussions is brand new for me and sometimes I get tripped up. I don't always know the right thing to say but that doesn't mean I'm not on the same page with you. I'm just . . . still figuring out how to express it correctly." Ryker implores with me his turbulent ocean gaze and I easily fall into his depths.

The pressure in my lungs disintegrates. "So, you're excited? And willing to check it out with me?"

"You know I'll go anywhere with you. I've already told you that."

"Well, I know but this would be a bit more . . . permanent. I don't expect you to move your entire life for me. Especially when this," I gesture between us, "is just starting. I'd understand if—"

He cuts me off. "You're my life, Sunshine."

Shivers race up my arms before settling in my heart.

"Are you cold?" Ryker asks while leaning closer.

I shake my head. "No, I'm blissfully warm. You always say the perfect thing. Don't ever worry about screwing up. I love that nickname so much." I fan my face to ward off the threat of pesky tears.

"I'm glad because that's what you are. Bright sunshine that breaks up the darkness inside of me." His tender tone reaches deep inside my lonely soul.

A dopey smile covers my lips as I shift forward. "You're Seek because I'll always find you." At least when he wants me to. "I'm glad you're willing to come with me but what about your job? I mean, if you have one. It's totally cool if you don't." My face heats with that silly assumption.

Ryker chokes but it almost sounds like a sharp chuckle. "It's a job I can do from anywhere so location isn't an issue. I work mostly at night. Nothing too interesting." His eyes slide away from me and my gut cramps with concern at the evasive reaction.

"Can you tell me what you do?" I coax after the server places our steaming dishes down.

"I'm a . . . hacker." He says the last word so quietly, I almost miss it.

"Like, breaking into computers and stealing information?"

Ryker snorts. "Or something. I'm actually a White Hat these days, which means my hacking is the good kind. I built and now maintain a software program that a few big companies use to keep Black Hats, the bad hackers, out."

"That's actually really interesting. It sounds like a secret society." The grin lifts my voice when he looks at me. "I'm terrible with computers."

He fidgets with the silverware and his eyes narrow. "It's secret all right. And I work with all these people I never meet. It's all telecommunication with fake names. Definitely doesn't help my introverted personality but it's what I'm good at."

"Have you been doing it for long?"

"Ever since I got my first computer in middle school. Coding and encryption always came natural to me," Ryker mumbles and seems uncomfortable.

"Does talking about this bother you?"

"Not specifically. It's just difficult to talk about myself. I'd rather talk about you."

I catch a glimpse of his arctic irises from under his lids.

Suddenly I remember something that he might understand. "All right. How about something that involves me and hacking? The night David was messing with me, suspicious charges showed up on my credit card. Could someone easily do that from a computer? Without having all my information?" Ryker goes pale and I worry that my question came out wrong. "It turned out to be nothing but I'm still curious," I add softly.

He groans and his gaze swings to the ceiling.

"I'm fucking up all over the place."

"What do you mean?" I ask while clasping his hand tighter.

Ryker coughs before admitting, "I alerted your bank, or rather my friend did that night. I didn't know what else to do without busting into your studio and dragging him out. Setting up unusual spending without actually touching your account is rather easy and easy to execute. That was the simplest way of getting you out of there on short notice. It gave you a believable excuse." The veins in his neck pop and his tone drags dangerously low.

"Hey," I murmur softly and reach for Ryker's other hand. He gives it to me before his distressed stare returns to me. "I'm all right because you saved me. That night could have been far worse. Nothing bad happened and I have you to thank." Sincerity bleeds from my words.

"I'm sorry for scaring you with the bank though. I didn't want to upset you."

His rough fingertips drag against my smooth skin and the contrast gives me goosebumps. The buckle from his bracelet glimmers in the overhead light and pride swells within me. I finally gave him something in return and that one piece is just a start.

A smirk dents my cheek. "I felt better afterwards just because you brought me coffee and a bagel. And left me a sweet note. You protected me and that's what means the most. It doesn't matter to me what method you used, coding versus confrontation. It's the fact you stepped in when most wouldn't have." I slowly blow out a lungful of air. "I'm sorry for bringing it up, Ryker. This evening should be happy and fluffy and fun."

"Never be sorry, Lennon. I'm the only one who should apologize."

"Should we change the subject? What should we plan next? Maybe the water park or zoo or–"

"MAKE IT RAIN!"

"What the heck?" I ask as our heads simultaneously twist toward the loud exclamation in the lounge area. Three women are sitting on stools at the middle of the large oak bar top laughing loudly. The girl in the middle raises a shot glass before once again yelling, "Make it rain!" A bartender walks by the trio and tosses a stack of cocktail napkins in the air, and they all bust into hysterics all over again.

Ryker mutters, "Looks like they're having a blast."

"Maybe we should do a shot. I've never done that. Have you?"

"Nope," he scoffs before shaking his head. "But I say let's do it. A little more booze won't hurt. It'll give us a reason to sit here longer while the effects wear off." Ryker slides the drink menu toward me. "Pick your poison."

I peruse the offerings quickly before my sight snags on one liquor. "Tequila? Lucy always drinks it."

Ryker shrugs and says, "Whatever you choose."

We signal the server and he makes quick work of our request. After a few minutes, he's back with overflowing shot glasses. "Lime and salt?" he asks while gesturing to the tray.

I nod and glance at Ryker. "The works? Might as well for our first time."

He grins before biting his lip. "Hopefully it tastes good."

The server laughs while walking away but we don't question him. I search Ryker's unwavering gaze and lift my drink while he raises his. We clink the rims together in a quiet cheers before simultaneously announcing, "Make it rain."

We both start coughing loudly as the liquid fire burns down our throats. I gag as the liquor threatens to make a reappearance but clamp my lips while swallowing several times.

"Holy shit," I sputter.

"That was fucking brutal," Ryker adds.

"First and last tequila shot?"

He scrubs a hand over his mouth before saying, "Making it rain was a bad idea."

"But at least we have the story to tell." I laugh at his slightly green complexion but my skin tone probably matches.

We finish the rest of our meal with easy conversation as all hints of alcohol leave our systems. Crumbs from a giant piece of chocolate cake we shared linger on the plate between us as Ryker pays the bill. He guides me to his truck with a gentle hand on my back before opening the passenger door for me. He leans in for a gentle kiss on my cheek that leaves the skin blushing bright.

My stomach sinks as we arrive at the apartment building and

walk toward my door. I don't want our date to end but it's almost midnight. At least Ryker doesn't have far to go to his own place.

Effing wild.

All this time, he's been living right next door. The surprises keep popping up but nothing has caused the terrified tremors I typically get around men. Even when he pushes limits and boundaries, my heart and mind trust him. Ryker is different and I accept his unusual methods of persuasion.

Someday I'll tell him how much he turns me on.

I turn to face him before dragging him close with our connected hands. "I had the best time tonight. Thanks for taking me to Mustavoe's. Their cheesy mac was fantastic," I whisper while looking into his sparkling blues.

"Best first date ever," Ryker murmurs before pressing his forehead to mine.

I lift my chin as my pulse triples. "More dessert?"

Ryker groans and softly caresses my lips with his. I roll up on tiptoes for more and he opens his mouth eagerly. My arms wrap around his shoulders as he strokes up my legs. Our tongues mesh in an erotic curl, gently curving and gliding together. I can taste a bite of spearmint from his gum but mostly it's sweet and sinful like pure sugar. His hands roam up my hips before dipping beneath my waistband. I moan into him as his seeking fingers skim along my lower back. Ryker bumps us into the wall before yanking me deeper into his body. Every inch of him is solid and meant to defend, just the way I love it. I rock into him slightly, my core ruling my brain, as my nails dig into his scalp. Ryker sucks on my bottom lip, adding more pressure as he starts pulling away. He releases my tender flesh with a wet pop.

"Fuck, you're so sexy." His breath is cool along my mouth.

"Then why did you stop?" I playfully pout.

The lust lapping my veins instantly chills with his reply.

"Sunshine, before we go any further, there's something you need to know."

fourteen

RYKER

The darkness is strong, a mighty beast set on ruin, but the light of day is just as powerful, if not more so. She'll be the one to prove it.

IT WAS AN IMPOSSIBLE DECISION to pull away from Lennon, particularly after she bumped her body against mine, but she deserves to know the truth. Her lovely blue-green gaze doesn't falter as she waits for me to speak. I breathe deep, asking for courage, hoping for understanding, but knowing I deserve nothing except contempt. Regardless of the consequences, I need to do right by Lennon.

I loosen my hold from her trim torso and reach for her hands. My tongue sticks to the dry roof of my mouth, as if I ate too much peanut butter. Lennon must notice my struggle because she speaks before I get shit figured out.

"It's okay, Ryker. I know what you're going to say," she

whispers sweetly while gripping my fingers.

My eyes widen as I consider the possibility. "You do? How?"

"It's not that difficult to figure out and I'm actually really glad you're bringing it up. We should talk about this stuff. I mean those kisses are so . . . *hot.*" She bites her lip, which has me reeling for an entirely differently reason. "Our first time will be even more special if we take it slow."

"Holy shit, hearing you talk about sex is so fucking distracting." I clench my eyes shut before groaning.

A bright red flush races up Lennon's neck before settling on her cheeks.

"Uh huh. It's fun to think about, right? But wait, distracting from what?"

"There's something else I need to say and it most definitely doesn't involve us getting naked. Unfortunately," I mutter as the mood between us shifts. "Can we go inside for a moment?" As my chin juts toward the door, she lifts a brow then nods before unlocking the deadbolt.

"Want anything to drink?" Lennon asks as she saunters into the living room.

"No, thanks. I don't need a reason to delay the inevitable." My conscience barrels forward, determined to give Lennon the truth, while my heart thunders with concern.

"Um, okay. Wanna sit down?"

I take a seat next to her on the couch and rub my clammy hands together. Lennon turns to face me but my nervous gaze keeps darting to the colorful walls.

"Please don't be mad. I swear this wasn't me being an asshole . . . or anything." I blurt as my blood pressure shotguns from a barrel.

"Ryker? What's going on? You can tell me anything." Her calm seeps into my chaos and I recline into the cushions. Her steady mood anchors me.

"I set up the studio space in Denten and paid for a portion to lower the rent." My voice is barely audible.

Lennon sucks in a gasp.

"Wh-what?" Her posture stiffens, shoulders tense and straight. "Why would you do that? I didn't need help with money." Her tone cracks, fracturing my courage to admit everything. She claps a palm over her mouth before shaking her head. "That came out harsher than I meant," Lennon mumbles between fingers. "But what the hell, Ryker? I don't understand."

My chest cinches, knowing my words need to spill fast.

"I completed the interest form and submitted it for you. The listing was another site you frequently visited so I found it that way. The rent was steep, especially for a small town, so I wasn't sure if that was holding you back." My pitch is practically a rasp as I push forward. "Based on the number of times you went to that page, this was something you really loved and my purpose is to make you happy."

Her jaw hangs open and her turquoise eyes bore into my soul. When Lennon stays silent, I take it as a hint to keep talking.

"The software I created is extremely profitable and the companies who use it pay me a small fortune. Money isn't important to me. I make a lot, spend a little, and want to give everything to you. This is a way I can provide for you." My tone wobbles when Lennon's posture stiffens. My muscles coil tight, ready to snap.

She exhales heavily.

"Okay, let's stop for a minute. This is not a turn I thought our evening would take." Her palm rests against her forehead. "I'm not really sure how to react. This is a pretty big deal to me, Ryker. Why didn't you ask me first so we could talk about it? And you let me yammer on about it at dinner without saying a word?"

Lennon's fingers spear into her hair as she sputters, "My father always uses money as a weapon to get his way. I hate that control he forces on me and have been working hard to get out of his financial grasp. I don't need your money and didn't need you to swoop in to pay for a lavish loft, whether it was an amazing spot or not. I've been saving for a while and was going to get a place within my budget."

My hackles rise at her defensive tone.

"I know you can do this on your own, Lennon. I've been watching you succeed independently for years and I wasn't trying to suggest you couldn't. *Fuck.*" My fists jam into my eye sockets while I attempt to keep her sunshine under my skin. "I'm screwing shit up left and right. I've done too much behind your back, and I know it's wrong, but that was the only way for me. And with a few clicks on the keyboard, it was a done deal. Splitting the rent with you was an easy choice, another big gift," I explain while watching for her reaction, my stomach sinking like a rock.

"Wow, there was a better way to go about this." She bites down on her lip. "I'm so grateful for all you do and extremely happy we've been hanging out. This situation is making me a tad frazzled so now isn't a great example but . . . *Urgh.* It's very important to me that I'm able to pay for my own way. After my parents tried keeping me home by offering loads of cash to start what they consider a pipe dream, I became determined to prove them wrong. There's not much I've been able to control so this is important to me."

There's lead weighing me down as I nod slowly, my face

holding no expression. Lennon sighs.

"You want to share the cost? Help me get a stellar studio? Let's talk about it. You were a secret for years but we're finally out in the open. I don't want to hide anything. I need you to trust me and tell me what's on your mind rather than finding out this way," she says as she shifts closer.

"I didn't want to lose you." My shoulders slump.

Lennon sets her palm on my knee and the connection pauses the turmoil raging inside me. When tension seizes my limbs, she squeezes my thigh.

"You make me feel so good, Ryker. Everything you do, I know it's for my benefit. Wanting me to have the most beautiful workspace ever? That's really sweet, and I'm sure your intentions were in the right place, but outright paying for a large chunk of something reminds me of my dad. I just wish this wasn't done in secret." My brain jams on the comparison to her father as she continues. "I like you, *a lot*, and this is new for us. I'm sure you weren't doing this to control me. I haven't told you much about my parents or the issues with them. Compared to the watching and following, maybe the money stuff shouldn't be an issue. But it is to me."

Her fingers massage my leg but I'm caught in the murky midnight blurring the edges of my vision. I don't want to leave Lennon but the comfort of the familiar darkness calls to me.

How do I fix this?

Do I apologize until she forgives me? Give her another present? Kiss her senseless? Tell her how gorgeous she looks in the low lamplight? Ask if I can run my fingers through her glossy dark hair? Go home so I don't make the situation worse?

I'm off balance and sliding all over with uncertainty. I'll do anything to turn this conversation around and get back on Lennon's good side.

"I don't know what to say," I mutter.

Way to go, genius.

"I want this to work out between us, Ryker. I'm not trying to be a brat and make this uncomfortable but it's important we talk through this." Lennon peers into me. The cold attacks my system as frost filters in but my heart keeps pumping warmth into my trembling limbs. My nails claw at the velvety fabric beneath me in an attempt to stay grounded.

"I've pushed too far and now you're going to leave." My lifeless words tumble out.

Lennon's head snaps back and she blinks rapidly.

"What? No, Ryker. Why would you say that? We're all right and I'm not angry, but you've gotta change tactics. I've never dated and don't know what's the best approach so please don't get upset. I just," she releases a deep breath, "don't want to be a naïve fool that keeps overlooking significant things. I realize everything you've done has been solely for either my protection or happiness but still. Even you said it seems like constant confession time and that doesn't sit right with me. There shouldn't be a reason to come clean. I don't think that's asking too much . . . or maybe it is? I'm screwing this all up."

Lennon pulls away before huffing loudly and losing her touch is catastrophic. My temples throb while my stomach quakes and I swallow hard to keep the nausea from building. I try to focus on her voice but suddenly my senses are spinning. My face tips down while I slam my eyes shut, trying to escape the madness. My soul begs for control but the insanity is waking up.

I won't go back to being alone. I can't.

"Ryker? Are you alright?" Lennon's healing melody crashes through the fog.

I glance at her through a thin crack in my lids before shaking my head. I manage to mutter a pathetic, "I'm sorry," through my strangled windpipe.

Lennon brushes along the leather wrapped around my wrist and the slight movement sends shocks up my arm. "It's okay, I'm not mad. That studio is my dream and you wanted to make it come true, which I can't fault you for. It's extremely romantic that you wanna take care of me. I love that, alright? It was a shock at first but what you did is different than how my parents handle things. Next time, let's decide together. This relationship stuff is a work in progress for me too." Her chuckle falls flat when she glances at my face. "Can you tell me what you're thinking? *Please?* I didn't mean to talk so much. For some reason, you bring out a blabbing side of me."

"You can't help me." My reply is hoarse.

"Ryker, don't say that. Everything is alright. Did I say something that bothers you? Can we talk about it? Let me be here for you, like you're always there for me. We can lean on each other," she says softly.

"You don't want to depend on me, Lennon. I'm a grown man incapable of figuring this shit out on my own. I'm trying to be better but it's not fucking working," I spit fury. "Wanna know the truth? I'm full of hate and darkness and disgusting memories that haunt me. You're the first and only person who's noticed me, by some unbelievable miracle, but my screwed-up mind won't stop making mistakes. Even though you're everything to me, I can't be better for you. And you deserve better than me. You should be with someone . . . *normal.*" That last word is sour in my ashy mouth and the roiling in my gut returns.

What the hell am I supposed to do now?

I stumble to my feet and start pacing. Lennon stands too but remains in one spot, watching me meltdown like a freak. The shadows are calling, tempting me with quiet isolation where this trouble doesn't exist. The shadows are sucking me back in and I'm letting them. This downward spiral could stop if my brain quits playing tricks but at this point, it was too late.

"Please stop. Why are you saying such awful stuff? Don't you want to be with me?" Lennon calls out.

"Because I'm a fucking loser, Lennon. I can't do anything right," I growl.

Her hand flies up to her mouth. "That's not true. You've done so many wonderful things for me. All the extravagant gifts, sweet notes, bagels and coffee, keeping me safe all these years, and so much more. Don't put yourself down like that."

Lennon's words are meant to be soothing but all I hear is static. Each syllable is another reminder of how weird I am, a list of necessary improvements. "Anything good has been wiped away by this."

"Please don't twist my words, Ryker. Money has been a touchy subject for me so I reacted poorly at first. After hearing why you paid for part of the studio, I realize how different this is compared to shit with my dad. Next time—" I'm too far gone to listen.

"There won't be a next time!" I roar. "You're going to leave because I'm a fucking freak, just like everyone always said. Fuck!" My muscles strain to silence the poison in my system and my feet stomp restlessly on the floor.

"Stop yelling at me! How did this get turned around so you're mad at me?" She wails loudly, freeing me from the debilitating chains.

My frantic movements come to a sudden stop as I face Lennon. She has tears streaming down her flushed cheeks and her chest is shuddering wildly. The inky black fades from my sight as her trembling sunshine pours through.

"No. No, no, no. I could never be mad at you. I'm furious at myself, for the stupidity and defects that make me an asshole. Everything is getting ruined because I'm not a normal fucking person," I thunder loudly as my hands ball into painful fists.

"Nothing is ruined, Ryker. We're okay. Let's take a timeout for a moment," her tone wobbles as she swipes at her wet face.

"Please don't leave me. I'll do better. I'm so sorry. Please forgive me." My voice cracks as the tension seeps out of my system. I'm shaking my head so fast, Lennon is a blur in front of me.

Lennon shuffles forward, tearing through the madness swirling around me.

"I'm not going anywhere, Ryker. You're wonderful and amazing and everything I've always wanted, remember? Don't ever doubt that." Her upper half deflates with a huge exhale. "This is just a little spat, like a . . . lover's quarrel." She traces her fingers down my trembling hand. "We hash it out, make up, and move on. Just because we have a tiff doesn't mean this is over between us. I hear this sort of thing happens all the time with couples." Her shoulders bounce as her nose wrinkles.

"I never want to fight with you." I expel the fiery chaos searing my lungs.

"This is just another first we had to experience. Sometimes arguments are necessary to work through the tougher stuff. That was mostly just flapping chaps and figuring stuff out." She explains.

"I want to impress you and don't know how. I've been wrong my entire life and never stood a chance of proving otherwise. I'm different and there's no changing that."

"I feel the same way, Ryker. That's why what we have is special, because we're different. Something no one else will understand, but maybe that's the best part. What's normal anyway? This is a major stepping stone, right? We'll keep learning together." Her beaming smile chases away the last storm clouds hovering on the edges of my vision. Lennon is the only one who can drag me from the darkness and keep me safe from the shadows.

I just have to let her.

"Okay," I murmur. "Together. We have a lot of adventures ahead." I manage a semblance of a smile and Lennon's laughter lifts my lips into a full grin.

"I can't wait for whatever comes next," she whispers like these experiences are our little secret—and maybe they are.

A large yawn escapes her before she's able to catch it. I glance at the clock and notice it's past one in the morning.

"It's late. Time for bed?"

Lennon nods before walking me out.

"Even with the bumps, this was one of the best nights I've ever had. Thank you for everything."

I couldn't agree more as my lips peck her satin cheek.

"See you soon, Sunshine."

After the lock clicks shut and she's safe, I turn toward my place. At the last minute, I decide to leave her something to find in the morning. I slide the yellow paper through the crack after scrawling a quick note. As I'm straightening to go, the door swings open and Lennon flings herself into my waiting arms.

"I'll never give up on you, Ryker. Don't worry," she murmurs against my neck.

Lennon gives me all the faith I need.

We're gonna be just fine.

fifteen

LENNON

HOW CAN SO MUCH HAPPEN in less than two weeks?

Since that first date with Ryker, the other aspects of my life have been taking center stage. My budding relationship was placed on pause while my all was dedicated to graduating and finishing the college. The time we've spent together since that night hasn't been nearly enough for my liking but the distance was unavoidable. Plenty of long chats and fun days wait around the corner. That will all happen soon enough when it's *just us.*

All summer long, and hopefully well beyond that.

I glance at my diploma on the counter and take a moment to appreciate the significance. That fancy piece of paper acknowledges four years of hard work and I'm prepared to put my freshly minted skills to good use. The professors set me free with a stack of recommendation letters, a bundle of real world advice, and the best wishes for starting my own business. The only unfinished business is the logo contest. The winner won't be announced until later this month but my abstract sunrise design made it into the final round so . . . *fingers crossed.*

"Did your parents finally leave?" Lucy asks as she rolls another suitcase into the living room, effectively popping my haze.

I groan at the mention of my mom and dad, clingy and bossy as ever.

"Yes, thankfully. Although they put up a decent fight, especially when they found out I was moving further away."

Of course, my overbearing parents tried corralling me back to their house but I refused before my dad could finish. When I told them about the studio space in Denten, they were not impressed. The protruding vein on my mother's forehead pulsed with worry as my father did everything in his manipulative power to convince me our hometown had better options. I swatted away their concerns and hugged them tight.

The old me could have been swayed but my backbone has strengthened recently, thanks to a certain someone. I'm a grown-ass woman, very capable of making my own choices, and need to start standing up for myself. That extends to situations with Ryker too. Although in a very particular setting, I wouldn't mind him bossing me around a little. Fire laps at my cheeks just thinking about him that way.

"Thinking of someone special? Do mommy and daddy dearest know Seeky-poo is planning to shack up with you?" Lucy laughs.

My eyes bulge.

"Heck no! Are you crazy? Even at twenty-two years old, I'm

still a little girl to them. Boys are not allowed within fifty feet. Can you imagine? They'd drag me back to Kentville kicking and screaming if they found out."

"I hear ya. Plus, dating him behind their back is extra sexy. Makes it all forbidden and hot." Lucy gnashes her teeth while growling but her silly gestures are lost on me.

My gut twists at the mention of keeping Ryker hidden, for several reasons. It's not that I'm embarrassed of him, quite the opposite, but my parents are freakishly overprotective. One look at my bulky boyfriend and I'd be shipped to a convent no doubt. If they ever knew about the watching . . . I've had enough secrets lately to last a lifetime but keeping Ryker from my parents is different though. At least, I think it is.

"Yeah . . . I'd much rather have typical parents that would accept their daughter dating. How will I ever bring him over to meet them? Do I wait until we're thirty?" The idea is maddening. "They should be glad I've found someone who makes me happy," I complain.

"Stop worrying so much, Lenny. Just enjoy this time alone with him. Don't look a gift horse in the mouth or whatever." She brushes my worry away with a sweep of her hand and a toss of her blonde hair over her dainty shoulder.

"I guess. Just doesn't seem right," I reply around the lump in my throat.

After my complicated argument with Ryker about always being honest, I'm feeling like the worst hypocrite.

My bestie sashays to me before clutching my hands. "Lenny, you've gotta follow your heart. You're an amazing designer and destined to do great things. Don't let your parents or Ryker or anyone else get in your way. Do you!" Lucy punctuates with a light tug on my fingers.

I shake loose from her grip and loop my arms around her shoulders. "Thank you. I couldn't ask for a better friend, even when you're a diva."

She giggles at my whispered words but I'm serious. This girl saved my ass from years of loneliness.

"You won't even miss me with that stud muffin occupying your time. Even though my creeper-sense went off at first, I've come to realize you're in good hands with that man. I'm going to come back and you'll have run off with him to the rainforest, living in total isolation like Jane and Tarzan." Lucy pulls back and rolls her eyes.

"That better not be a bad joke about—"

"Calm down, Lenny. It wasn't a personal knock against him or anything." Lucy gives me a wide-eyed stare. "Just be careful, okay? I'm not ready to be an auntie."

My mouth drops open in horror.

"Are you serious right now?"

"Safe sex, Lenny. Use protection," she explains while patting me on the head like a child.

I shove her hand away and huff, "I'm still on the pill, per your advice freshman year."

"Excellent. Good stuff, right? Keeps Aunt Flow in check, that cranky bitch." Lucy pops her lips and flicks her wrist. "But I'm talking about condoms. STDs, or sexually transmitted diseases for your virgin ears, are no joke. Unplanned pregnancy isn't the only side effect of bumping uglies."

"Why are we talking about this?" I groan while covering my flaming face.

"Because you two will be screwing like rabbits in no time

and it's my civil duty as your friend to provide the basics. Like, wrapping up his trouser snake." She imitates rolling a condom down her finger and my stomach bottoms out.

I shake my head and swallow the discomfort.

"Can we stop? Ryker and I have barely brushed the subject."

"Oh, you'll be groping it in no time."

"How are we friends?"

"Why do you always ask me that?" She gapes in mock offense.

"Moving on!" I hold up my palms.

"Not so fast. My Lyft will be here soon so any last discussion points before I'm an ocean away?" She asks as she moves to an unpacked pile of supplies. "Everything big that I'm not bringing is already in storage. I know you'll be out by July but maybe you could check on the place while I'm still gone?"

"As if you have to ask. I'll take care of whatever's left." A heavy sigh rushes from my lungs. "I can't believe you're leaving and we won't be living together anymore."

"Ah, don't get mopey on me. We already cried over ice cream last night."

"I know. This is just the end of an era or something. You're going to Europe. I'm moving to Denten. This summer will be totally different." I bite my tongue before deciding to ask Lucy for advice. "I have a question, and don't you dare make fun of me."

Lucy chuckles from her spot on the floor before stopping what she's doing to look up at me.

"I'll do my best to remain sass-free."

My hands wring together as I mumble, "You know I'm very inexperienced, and not just with boys. There's so much I've missed out on with life in general thanks to my bubble-wrapped childhood. What are some fun activities regular people have done by our age? I'm planning a summer of firsts, for Ryker and me." I cringe at my word choice, knowing he'd probably go ballistic hearing me refer to us as anything but normal.

"Like a bucket list?" She tilts her chin while squinting at me.

I chew on that term for a moment.

"Well, kind of. I'm thinking more along the lines of typical stuff, not just crazy adventures to check off before we die." I shudder. "You know, easy things like bowling," I repeat the example I used to lure Ryker into this plan.

"You haven't gone bowling?" She squeaks. "Wow. Um, all right. I get where you're going with this. Sex is number one though, right?"

My gaze sweeps skyward as I ask for patience. "You're impossible. Forget I asked."

Lucy snickers.

"If you weren't so easy to mess with, my life would be horribly boring. All right, for real, this is super freaking cute. You'll have to send pictures. How about The Sculpture Garden?"

I nod while grabbing my notepad and urge her to keep going.

"The zoo? Waterpark? Oooh, you should visit some dunes and cliffs. What about an aquarium?" She keeps going as my imagination runs rampant.

"Yeah, these are all really great. Do you have any date spots?" I ask while scribbling everything down.

"The bedroom?" she suggests with humor lacing her tone. "Lenny, look. You're barking up the wrong tree with this sugary sweetness. I've done my best to point you in the right direction but don't drag me into this romance nonsense. This girl," Lucy points to herself, "is single, twenty-two, and headed to Paris. I'm not interested in cuteness. You've got it handled, I have total faith.

Look at that killer list." She juts her chin at my paper.

I smirk as she gives me fish-lips. "Thanks, Luc. I'll hopefully make you proud. Anything you need help with last minute?" I offer while she puts the final items in her duffle bag.

"How about a glass of wine? All this cheese has made me thirsty," she tosses out while walking toward the fridge.

We sit at the table and talk about nothing until her ride arrives. I hug Lucy tight while trying not to cry and she promises to call after landing. With weepy eyes, I watch her strut out of our apartment as she heads off to one of the most famous French design houses.

I hope they're prepared.

I console myself by glancing down at my notepad. Nineteen awesome ideas mark the page and I'm eager to share all of them with Ryker in the months ahead. Excitement prickles down my spine while I picture the discovery of all these firsts. As my mind twirls to more . . . *intimate* activities, the prickling bursts into scorching heat that streaks to my lower belly.

As if hearing my thoughts, a knock echoes into the room. I grab the list and bound over with a spring in my step. I fling open the door, revealing a delicious Ryker leaning against the wall.

"I'm getting ready," blurts out before I yank him inside.

Oh wow, is my voice breathy?

A soft rumble vibrates up his chest. "For what?"

"Everything."

sixteen
RYKER

Real monsters prefer the black of night, hell-bent on ruin and destruction. All I want is sunshine and light, so what does that make me?

WHEN LENNON BITES HER LIP and whispers *everything*, it sounds like a sinful invitation. I mentally switch gears and focus on *those* implications. My intentions had been respectable when I knocked on the door but her turquoise orbs are full of naughty suggestion. She's decimating my plans with one word. The filthy thoughts fueling my lust-addled mind makes everything below my belt tighten noticeably. I shift from one foot to the other, trying not to draw attention to my sudden discomfort.

"What does, um, *everything* mean?" I somehow find just enough braincells to choke out the question.

Lennon hums, "Wanna see?"

Is she serious?

Holy shit, do I ever.

My teeth grind together as a strangled moan trips off my tongue. What's gotten into her? I thought we were going to talk about the barrier that's been holding me back from opening up. The bullshit from my past caused an epic freak out after our first date and I don't want that happening again. But if Lennon wants to hold off for another few hours and explore other options, I'm definitely not going to deny her.

All I do is nod like an idiot and wait for . . . what I'm not sure. Lennon can take charge of this portion of the evening. When she shoves a piece of paper at me with a wide smile, my burning arousal immediately loses steam. She's clearly been working on our list and the entire page is full of her flowing script. I want to smack my head for leading the charge into horny asshole territory when that's obviously not what's on Lennon's mind.

My eyes sweep slowly down her ideas and I'm not surprised to discover these are all new activities for me. I'm about to compliment her efforts when she tugs me over to the couch.

"I've missed you, Ryker. Thanks for coming over," she says while plopping down on the fluffy cushions.

I sit next to her before placing a soft kiss on her silky cheek.

"I missed you too," I echo. "But I'm always around. I saw you yesterday at graduation. Congratulations again." I'll never forget the sight of her brilliance lighting that stage as she accepted her diploma. Everything within me was cheering for her even if my mouth remained sealed shut.

"I knew you were there but it's not the same when we can't talk. I want you to be part of the celebration," Lennon pouts and my stomach fills with bricks at the thought of her unhappiness.

Our fingers lace together.

"I'm sorry, Sunshine. It's not the same when other people are around but I'm trying to get better. Yesterday I would have embarrassed you by being awkward and uncomfortable. It was better for everyone that I kept my distance, especially with your parents around."

"They're the ones who need to be better." Lennon scowls. "I shouldn't be terrified to have my boyfriend around for something so important."

My gut twitches at her title for me. She looks directly into my soul as she continues, "I'd never be embarrassed of you, Ryker. I hope you know that. If I had my way, you'd be around everywhere I go." Her accepting words sounds like music to my warped spirit, wiping away years of torment.

"I want that too. Very much. But it's not that easy," I admit with a sigh. "I've been this way my entire life."

"You've never met anyone else that put you at ease?" she asks quietly.

My head shakes slowly as bitterness loops around my rib cage. "I don't talk to people, Lennon." My head shakes slowly. "It's been far easier to remain silent, aside from the chicken scratch notes needed to get my point across or ordering coffee and a bagel or unintelligible grunts while confronting some asshole. That hasn't changed since I was young. I don't like them looking at me, judging me, thinking they know something about me, ready to fling useless advice my way on how to be like everyone else. It's exhausting being constantly scolded and picked apart so I locked everyone out."

Lennon's warm palm slides along my cool wrist when she moves closer.

"It's not easy for me either and never has been. Mostly because my parents taught me to fear everything with a pulse, especially boys. If it weren't for Lucy, who they barely approve of, I'd be socially isolated. I didn't know what a real friend was until college." She offers a sheepish shrug. "It hasn't been an easy road but it's getting better each day. I'm glad you can talk to me."

"You're very different for me," I explain easily. "I've never felt the desire to be around others, probably because my own parents shunned me. Made me believe human contact was totally overrated considering I survived the first eighteen years of my life virtually alone. But then you walked into homeroom." My lips quirk up at the corners, recalling that monumental moment. "You changed my life that day, without even realizing it. Have you ever felt something like that? Suddenly it all makes sense? The suffering and torment is worth it?"

Lennon's eyes get hazy, as if she's lost to her memories.

"Yeah, I know exactly what you mean." Her voice sounds far away even though she's right here with me. "When I walked into that classroom and sat in front of you, nothing else mattered. I clearly did a crappy job showing you but those hours spent near you, silent or not, meant so much to me. I was devastated after school ended, figured I'd never see you again." Her gaze clears as she searches my features. "Luckily that wasn't the case, right? The universe tilted and brought us together, two awkward oddballs."

I can't control the disdain from locking up my muscles as she uses those words, a deeply ingrained habit. My mind has been strictly instructed to reject the concept of being different, even though I'm well aware of how unusual I actually am. Lennon shouldn't have to deal with someone flawed and strange but this is me—ab-fucking-normal.

She twists toward me and rests her free hand on my thigh.

Our linked fingers find a spot on her knee, which bumps up to my hip. We're touching enough to quiet the riot boiling in my blood but Lennon has picked up on my mood.

"Can we talk about the issue with being different?" she whispers quietly but her question slams into me like a wrecking ball.

My torso ripples with increasing strain. "Who really wants to stand out, Lennon?" The comeback is a harsh crack in the quiet room and I mutter a soft apology immediately after. "It's painful to dredge up the garbage in my past, but I'll do it for you. Maybe leaning on each other won't be so bad?" I whine like a baby, that's what this shit does to me as I'm dragged into the rotten memories of my childhood that should never be relived.

"I didn't mean to force you into this, Ryker. If it's that awful, we don't have to talk about the past. I just thought," she shrugs before her eyes boomerang around the room, "it might be helpful to share the hurt with someone."

A wheeze climbs my cinched windpipe.

"No one else would *ever* get this out of me, but you're the only person who matters. If this sheds some light on why I'm fucked up, it will be worth it."

Lennon tries to interject as she grips my leg harder but I barrel forward. The rusty gate to my past has been flung open and the grime oozes from my voice.

"My mother and father are the worst type of people, they don't deserve to be considered parents. Having a child should be a cherished blessing, but to them, I was the bane of their existence. They never let me forget it either. From my earliest memory, maybe four or five years old, their only interactions with me were insulting." The misery leeches out as my breathing falters. Lennon gulps loudly before scooching closer, giving me her warmth and the strength to continue. "Most of the time, they wouldn't bother putting their hands on me. Their preferred method of torture was vicious verbal lashings that cut deeper than any knife could. Day in and out, they told me I was different and weird and stupid. It was all my fault for being unlovable. If only I could have been *normal*, none of that would have happened. They would have treated me like parents are supposed to. They were neglectful and cruel to the worst degree. Even basic needs were my responsibility since they couldn't waste precious time feeding or bathing a worthless mooch. The only saving grace was they were rarely home since drugs and alcohol were their babies." I shudder as goosebumps cover every inch of chilled my flesh. It's been a long time since I've seen their faces but the memories appear vivid, like a fresh wound yet to heal.

My voice is robotic as I unravel further. "By the time kindergarten started, I was already tarnished. The odds were stacked against me from the start but it was more than that too. I always assumed something was . . . *off* with me but couldn't explain it. I didn't talk or like looking at others, even the softest touch felt like hot pokers on my skin. My stomach was always a tangle of painful knots, a ticking time bomb following me around. I was constantly looking over my shoulder, believing something was out to get me so each moment was a battle."

Fat droplets drip down Lennon's cheeks as she openly cries, not bothering to hide her sorrow. Maybe hers can do the healing mine never could. I tug Lennon closer and she effortlessly collapses against my chest. She gives me strength I never had back then.

"I only went to school for hot meals and to escape my house," I start again. "Teachers did their best but no one was willing to put in any real effort to reach me, not that it would work anyway.

The other kids left me alone since I didn't bother anyone. We're all so egocentric at that age, you know?

"Around middle school, that all changed though." I blow out a deep breath while rubbing my buzzed scalp. "Overnight I became the target everyone sought out. The slight reprieve I'd been surviving in disappeared in a flash. Their taunts and names and jabs were continuous. Freak, moron, creep, loser, psycho, mental . . . Crazy Eyes. Endless and spiteful, day in and out. It didn't matter that I went out of my way to avoid them and didn't fight back. Maybe that was part of the issue, they all thought I was a spineless wimp for not defending myself."

Lennon sniffles and I rest my jaw on her silky hair, absorbing everything good she's emitting.

"The confusion and awkwardness turned into fury and anger. They tore me apart and I took it out on myself. Why did I let them do this? Why did I have to be different? Why couldn't I be normal, like them? If I wasn't so strange and awful, blending into the crowd would be easy. Instead I stuck out like a huge fucking blob, asking for ridicule. I began to wonder what the fucking point of living was. Why not make everyone happy and leave in a very permanent sense." Lennon gasps so I clutch her tighter.

"The next morning, you walked into homeroom and I found meaning. Just like that." My fingers snap and I allow the pain to fall away.

My heavy exhale ruffles her glossy locks, like shinny ripples swallowing the shadows.

"You were this perfect beam in all the murky filth I'd been wading through. At first glance, it clicked with me—you were someone I needed. I'd never connected to anyone else. Ever. These new feelings were frightening but I liked it. I clung to the light you gave me and let you pull me from solitary confinement like the greatest blessing. That's exactly what you were too. You saved me from a world of silence and hurt," I murmur against her temple before placing a soft kiss there. Lennon bands her arms around me and snuggles deep into the embrace.

This is what peace feels like.

"I greedily absorbed all the warmth reflecting off you. Just being close kept me sane and the pull wound tighter around me until I craved you. Knowing I'd see you the next day kept me breathing through the night. The entire time I was becoming addicted, you were completely oblivious to your monumental impact on my life. But you saw me," my whisper washes over Lennon and she trembles. "That first smile wrecked me in the best way, as if I wasn't already gone for you. I'd never be able to leave you alone but that afternoon with Jason changed the game. Suddenly it wasn't just about that unexplainable connection to you. My mind twisted into believing you needed my protection so keeping you safe became my purpose," I rasp while my eyes clamp shut, forcing away images of her in danger.

My forehead presses to hers.

"That's why I can't ever lose you, Lennon. This is why I cling and stalk and overstep and smother. I'm terrified of scaring you away yet my actions might push you in that direction regardless of what happens." My vision blurs as I whisper, "Never leave me. I can't go back to the shadows. I won't survive alone." It's unfair to place that weight on her shoulders but I can't help the plea from slipping out.

Our upper bodies mold together as we sit in silence, reflecting on my harsh history. My hands circle along her back while her fingers clutch the fabric at my ribs. Lennon's gentle movements course through me, my erratic heartbeat pounding against hers.

She tilts her face up until our lips barely brush, a soft slide of comfort. When we pull apart, Lennon's eyes are still weepy and I kiss away the tears. She clears her throat before murmuring, "I'm afraid to say anything without ruining the moment." Her torso expands with a large inhale. "I can't even . . . it's just completely . . ." she starts before pausing. "First of all, *thank you*. I'm sure that was extremely difficult but your trust means so much to me."

My breathing hitches while I blink rapidly to clear my vision. When she continues, the sugar in her typical tone is noticeably absent. "I'm furious and horrified and so damn upset that you were treated so poorly for that long. No one deserves to live like that, especially you. What they did is inexcusable. Every single person who's picked on you is a disgusting stain on society. I can't imagine what you went through or why you took any blame for what they did. How are your parents not in jail?" Lennon grinds out through clenched teeth.

"I never said anything or turned them in because the evil I knew was better than the unknown. Foster homes and the system were no better. My mother and father were horrible but at least I knew what to expect from them." Grit coats my mouth.

"You're a wonderful man with a beautiful soul and my life is so much better with you in it," Lennon's soothing words smooth my ragged edges.

My pulse jackhammers as I stare into her aqua gaze. "I can't believe you've agreed to date me, that you're my girlfriend. You've given me a life I never dreamed possible. I'm not battered by anxiety or brimming with hate. I'm . . . happy." I'm startled by the realization at first but the declaration gains momentum quickly as a real smile curves my lips. "For the first time, I feel normal. And it's all thanks to you."

Lennon's hiccupping sob snags my attention and my eyes expand at her fresh tears. "Gah, I'm crying again. Sorry, sorry," she apologizes while fanning her face. "You're so sweet, Ryker. I'm the lucky one, you have no idea. Together, we're our own normal. You get me and I understand you. We may not fit in with the masses but why would we want to? We get to be ourselves. I'm here, *with you,* because of who you are. We fit. No matter how anyone else defines us. Are you with me?" she asks while shaking my arms and bouncing in place.

"I'm always with you, no need to ask." My fingers stroke along her soft skin as I clear my throat. "How are you doing that? Just accepting me for who I am, after everything I've done?"

"Something deep inside me explains the how and why, like the purest gut instinct." Lennon taps her stomach. "I just know everything you did wasn't malicious or selfish or misguided. I'm your purpose and there's nothing better than that," she rapidly explains.

Joy blasts under my skin. "You're the greatest gift, Sunshine. I'll never take you for granted and will spend every moment cherishing all you give me." I feel like flying. "No more misery or sorrow, all right? We've had enough of that."

After a heavy exhale I ask, "What's first on our summer list?"

Lennon's eyes widen before she twists to snatch the discarded paper. She gives it a quick glance and chuckles.

"Mini golf."

An unexpected laugh bursts from me, a deep boom that echoes. The unfamiliar sound is foreign to my ears but makes complete sense for the occasion.

Well, there's another first.

seventeen

LENNON

After a life of nothing but heartache and desolation, he has it in him to laugh.

I SHAMELESSLY GAWK AS THE joyful sound expands around us, chasing away any lingering misery. My jaw drops further when his infectious tune grows louder, feeding my aching soul. My eyes devour every jolly shake from Ryker's muscular chest. Happiness explodes and spills over, soaking into my skin while stealing my breath. The moment stretches and swells until we're floating in a bubble of bliss, anything else blurs and fades into the distant background. Ryker laughing satisfies all senses, the epitome of a full body experience.

Is this real?

The paper crinkles in my trembling fist, calling attention to the journey ahead of us. Not just the one jotted down between the lines but the life we're slowly building together. Now is the time to celebrate what we've found despite it all. Our kindred spirits found each other, through years of pain and suffering alone.

I tuck my chin as my eyes mist for the billionth time this evening. I can't seem to clog the emotional spigot, especially with Ryker spoon-feeding me reasons to cry. Whether the situation calls for it or not, I've always shed tears easily, and he's probably thinking there's something seriously wrong with my stability.

Who else cries this much?

I roll my eyes at that silly thought, considering we just talked about comparing ourselves to others. When I glance up through wet lashes and find Ryker's lips tipped into a small smile, my concern melts away. He cares for me, weepy or not. I watch his calm ocean irises, content with the silence once the giggles taper off. His raw strength and power shines from every part of him, but I see it most from his glittering gaze.

"What do you see?" His whisper startles me from my trance.

"Paradise," I breathe, feeling weightless. "Everything good and right and meant to be." I blink a few times to clear my mind. "We're together on a tropical island with white sand and crystal-clear water waiting to provide comfort. The sun blazes down, toasting every bit of bare skin with a golden glow, giving limitless warmth. Gentle waves lap against the shore, offering loyal protection and devotion. Endless possibilities and freedom and . . . *you*," swirls from my lungs and I shiver slightly.

His Adam's apple bobs with a heavy swallow. "Is that island on there?" Ryker's voice is hoarse as he juts his chin to our list, being mercifully crushed by my hand. "Because I'd like to take you."

"I'm already there," I say smoothly.

The air shifts with my accelerating pulse, longing blankets the both of us. I tip closer, my palm over his pounding heart, before reaching to his flushed face. He smells spicy, like cinnamon candy, and I want to taste him. *Badly.*

Ryker's cool palm travels up to cup my fiery cheek. "Can I kiss you?"

"No need to ask," I reply and he pulls me into him.

Our noses bump and I giggle while his laughter puffs lightly against my lips. The amusement dissolves when his mouth touches mine, so delicately at first that I shiver from the tease. Ryker's tongue tickles along my bottom lip before exploring deeper. I shift higher to get a better angle and soon find myself straddling his lap. Our mouths fuse while hands wander willingly. My fingers drag up his neck into his cropped hair while his skim down my bare shoulders, goosebumps rising in his wake. Ryker's arms thread around my lower back, holding tight, as I rock against him. His body is taut, practically vibrating, as I nip his lower lip. I want to drive him crazy, exactly as he's doing to me.

Is it working?

Ryker groans into my mouth and I swallow the warm air like a drug. I ingest his pleasure greedily, wanting every drop he's willing to give. His flavor is intoxicating and my tongue strokes along his for another burst.

When he switches into another gear, Ryker rolls until we're falling flat on the couch. I bounce against the plush cushions and an unladylike *oomph* deflates my chest. We're about to topple over the edge when his palm slams to the floor, halting our clumsy descent.

"In my mind, that move was graceful as hell. Are you okay?"

I nod vigorously and pull his mouth back to mine.

Less talking, more touching.

Ryker grinds against me, leaving no space between us, while our slick lips slide together. His whole body is hard against me, his pecs firm and abs flexed in effort, not to mention what's rocking below his waist. I'm pushed deeper into the soft padding and my back bows, searching for more of him. My palms sneak under the hem of his shirt and beg for more.

Suddenly he rips his mouth from mine.

"Mini golf! We should get going." His rapid breathing matches my own.

"Pretty sure that can wait until later," I murmur while trying to yank him down. Ryker resists and lightly circles my wrists to loosen the tight grip on his shirt. I release him with a huff, not ashamed to be pouting. "I was having fun."

"And you think I wasn't?" He questions incredulously with a deep crease in his brow.

I squint and wrinkle my nose. "So, why did we stop?"

"I only have so much control, Lennon. I mean, look at you." Ryker blows out a heavy exhale as his sparkling eyes dart along my features. "You're my every waking dream laid out before me, but this isn't how our first time should be."

"There's other things we can do . . ." I begin to suggest when he cuts me off.

"I want to touch you, feel every part of you underneath my fingertips but not on the fresh grave of my past. I've put those memories to rest tonight but the ghosts just left," he explains carefully while rubbing along my forearms.

I scold myself as I look around as if I can see these invisible figures.

"You're right. I'm sorry. It's been a very emotional evening and we should get out of this space for a while. Mini golf, here we come." I smile and shimmy, trying to defuse the heat scorching my skin.

Ryker groans as he stands and tries adjusting himself secretly before helping me off the couch. While stretching, we take turns blushing while catching each other gawking at exposed slivers of flesh. I bite my lip, swollen from his kisses, before snatching up the list and my phone.

I smooth out the wrinkled sheet.

"We'll have to re-write this if it keeps getting tossed around. Or I can just put it in here." I wiggle the device in my hand.

"Nah, it's perfect like that. A few folds and bruises add appeal, right?" He flicks a crinkled corner and smirks. I realize the hidden meaning and my stomach flutters at the dimple piercing his stubbled cheek.

Our fingers lace as we head out, ready to try our luck at miniature golf. When I was in middle school, a group of popular kids would always spend Friday nights at the local putt-putt. I wasn't cool enough to get an invite, not that my parents would have let me go, but I was always curious what the fuss was about. That's why it was the initial activity I thought of when jotting down ideas. My teenage self is silently squealing and very pleased to finally uncover the secret.

"This place has great reviews and isn't too far away," I say while putting the address in my map app after we've climbed into Ryker's truck. We take off once the automated voice spits out directions and settle into compassionate silence.

My knee bounces wildly while I glance out the window, lost in random thoughts. I jolt slightly when Ryker's palm rests on my thigh.

"Nervous?" he asks.

I swing my startled gaze to him. "No. Why would I be? This is going to be fun, right?"

"That's kinda the point. Just making sure since you looked about ready to tuck and roll." He glimpses at me from the corner of his eye.

My chuckle bubbles out.

"Um, that's something I'm good with never attempting. Very funny, very funny." I lay my hand on his." I'm excited for this, that's all. Maybe a tad concerned about making a fool of myself but hopefully you'll be kind enough to let it slide."

Ryker snorts as he guides the vehicle around a sharp curve, following the robotic lady's commands. "Don't worry, Sunshine. I'm sure you're a natural."

We found out he was super wrong after my first choppy swing about thirty minutes later. The small neon ball zipped over the short wooden wall so fast I figured it was running scared. The next five holes had a very similar outcome. I would line up, or attempt to, but the club never glided across the green with ease and the ball shot to the stratosphere. An enormous decorative clown mocked me for missing a shot. A surprisingly realistic T-rex blew smoke from his nose when I failed to sink the putt into his castle, and it became very evident mini golf was not my game.

Bless his heart, Ryker kept a straight face while I huffed and puffed in frustration. This was all in the name of a good time but I was turning this fun-tivity into a travesty. At least my date was holding his own—and stopping me from doing any permanent damage to the course. When my shot on the sixth hole ricochets into the water, Ryker takes pity on me.

"Wanna quit? No one said we have to finish. Maybe we should grab ice cream or do something else." His lips quirk as his eyes twinkle.

I gasp and act affronted, over-the-top goading tone and all.

"My word, Ryker. Was that a joke? We're far past the point of no return. We're going all the way!" I exclaim while shaking my fist in a ridiculous fashion.

"Wow." Ryker shakes his head and bites his plump lip. "You're too adorable. C'mere," he says while tugging on my belt loop.

I sway into him without resistance as he dips down to my mouth. The kiss is chaste and quick but powerful all the same. Sparks erupt in my toes and travel up until the sensation zaps my scalp. I sag against him further, an effortless comfort cuddling around us like a favorite blanket.

Ryker nuzzles into my neck before gently brushing his lips along the sensitive skin. I shiver in his arms and stretch my throat to give him more room. He sweeps up to my ear before nipping the lobe.

"It's your turn," he whispers with a heated sigh.

My teeth clack together as I stiffen, remembering where we are. I push away from Ryker slowly, as if not to draw more attention from onlookers.

"Tease," I mutter as I bend to set up my tee.

"What was that, Sunshine?" he questions after I straighten.

"Oh, nothing at all. Just getting ready to win." I glance over my shoulder.

"You're asking for trouble."

"More like begging but whatever," I volley back.

"Why don't you take your shot?" Ryker motions to my club.

"I thought you'd help me, since you've got all the skills." Electricity buzzes under my skin as the lighter blue of his irises crashes into the darker edge.

"Maybe if you ask nicely."

I bite my lip before purring, "Please?"

His huge palms engulf my hips as he steps behind me, apparently set on assisting me with this shot or something else entirely. We both know what's really going on but I'll gladly play along.

My feet take a tiny shuffle backward as I wiggle in his hold.

"Now who's the tease?" Ryker's breath rushes across my nape. I almost moan. My entire body is like a match waiting to be lit and I have no clue what to do about that. My inexperience doesn't stop me from trying though.

"Wanna make things interesting?" I ask with my chin tipped to face him.

"What do you have in mind? That glint in your eye is kind of freaking me out," he admits while shifting away from my advances. "You're going to get me kicked out of here for public indecency so it better be clean fun."

I pout shamelessly, hoping it looks flirty.

"If I get the ball in, you give me a massage later. If I miss, you'll be the one getting a little rub down."

Ryker makes a strangled noise before coughing loudly. "Jesus, Sunshine." His voice is a hoarse rasp. "Seems like I win either way."

I smirk while lifting a coy brow. "Exactly."

eighteen

RYKER

Each day is a new experience that leaves me blissed out of my mind. I had no concept of what happiness could be.

SHE'S TEMPTING ME AGAIN.

It's been a week of this exquisite torture, a beautiful pull into her delicate web. Ever since that massage after golf, which I gladly guaranteed she received, my control has been tested and stretched beyond feasible limits. When I picked up that golf ball and tossed it in the hole, a chain reaction of delicious enticement began. Sunshine has been playing with fire and I'm not sure how much more I can take before taking the plunge.

When we went to the zoo, Lennon tucked tightly against me while looking at the exhibits. At the aquarium, she lured me into hidden corners with promises of stolen kisses. I'll never forget her overtly seductive strut each time she got up to bowl, suggestive but subtle. Wandering touches that gave me goosebumps, lingering kisses that made my heart race, sweetly whispered phrases that left plenty to the imagination, shy glances with flushed cheeks . . . all tasty bait I gobbled up like gummy bears.

I've always known Lennon will be my first, if she's willing. Sharing my body with her has been my craving since she smiled at me and by now, I'm sure she feels the same way. The potential of those wicked fantasies becoming reality have me panicking.

The reluctance to take our relationship to a more physical level is solely due to sheer terror. My anxiety has been ratcheting up to dangerous degrees when I think of the thousand ways to fuck up. What if I hurt Lennon by being too rough? How do I make sure she has an orgasm? Will she still find me attractive naked? What if she isn't turned on enough? If I do something really wrong, will sex be ruined for her? I could blow it in countless ways—prematurely and just . . . in general. It's far too much for my already frazzled mind to manage.

At least we've gotten really good at making out and dry humping. Anything with her that close to me, even with layers of clothes in the way, is fucking mind-blowing. Those are hints of how it could be between us, the slight brushes of skin that leave me hard, aching, and boiling with desire. I never understood the term blue balls when the stupid jocks joked about it in school, but my clarity on the painful subject is extremely obvious now. The sexual frustration, and agonizing pressure in my groin, is worth it though.

Everything needs to be perfect for our first time—the most important first of all.

We're comfortable and compatible in ways I didn't know existed. I've already lost count of the number of times she's pointed out ridiculously accurate details about me that no one else would notice. If I didn't know better, I'd assume Lennon has been studying me over the years too.

Lennon is currently humming softly while draping fabric over a mannequin, her hips swaying hypnotically to a silent beat. We've been at her studio on campus most of the day, quietly working on separate tasks. I'm building a new software so hopefully neither of us will have to worry about money again. I'll have more than enough to make all of her wishes come true, which hopefully include me.

"I don't hear much typing going on over there, Mister Doxson," Lennon sing-songs before twirling behind the dress form.

A shiver passes through me while I imagine calling her the same name, except as my missus. It's way too soon for such visions but that doesn't stop my wild brain from diving into the future. Her graceful moves distract me further.

"Who do you dance for when you're by the window?" I blurt as my eyes lock on her delicate movements. My filter is even weaker than usual since my brainpower is being directed to keeping other areas in check.

"What do you mean?" She cocks her head my way. "I'm in the middle of the room and this is my typical flurry of artistic chaos." Lennon demonstrates by continuing to bounce around her creation.

"Not what you're currently doing," I start. "There were a few times when I was watching that it seemed like you were almost . . . putting on a show." I bust out the last part before nerves clamp my mouth shut.

Lennon's face turns a bright shade of red as she dips her chin. "Um," she bites her lip. "That's really embarrassing."

"Sorry, Sunshine." My nape burns with shame. "I didn't mean to make you uncomfortable. Just curious but forget I asked."

She shuffles over slowly as her gaze bounces around the open space, refusing to land on me.

"It's fine. I just feel really silly about it." Lennon takes a deep breath. "I caught on that someone was following me when the gifts started appearing in really convenient spots. There were several situations when I actually caught sight of a shadowy figure but you'd disappear just as quickly. This might sound super bizarre but I grew attached to the mere idea of having a secret admirer. There was a person out there who was infatuated and interested in me enough to do all this wonderful stuff, like leave sweet notes and my favorite coffee." She fidgets with a pin between her fingers. "When I was feeling a bit bold and picturing the mysterious stranger, who for whatever reason didn't scare me, my body would take charge. Thinking about *you* watching was exciting." Her words are soft and barely-there but I hear the meaning loud and clear.

My palm drags over the stubble covering my jaw. "Am I dreaming? How is this real life?"

Lennon hums and I pull her into my arms.

"You were really doing all that for me?"

Her head bobs again and my pulse pounds ferociously, echoing throughout my entire being.

She shifts slightly before peeking up at me. "I told you how special that attention makes me feel. My courage kept increasing as Seek became more obvious," Lennon murmurs through a smile. "I wanted to draw you closer and entice you. Having you watch was . . . *hot*," she exhales the ultimate invitation before burying her flushed face in my chest.

I groan loudly as my resistance frays to tattered strings. "Sunshine, you have no idea what that does to me."

Lennon bumps her hips into mine before edging even closer, rubbing along some very solid evidence.

"Pretty sure you're giving me a *big* hint. Why are you holding back, Ryker?"

My jeans become impossibly tight and delaying sex suddenly seems very stupid.

"I don't want to screw anything up. There's a lot of pressure, from *everywhere*, and I can't stand the idea of doing anything wrong for you." My hands tremble as they drift down her back.

"We can go slow. There's a few bases we haven't rounded yet. I don't want to race straight to the main event but we could do some other stuff first." Lennon's satiny voice cools the stress raging through my muscles.

I nod quickly, definitely following the direction she's taking. "O-okay. I like the sound of that."

"I mean, I've heard foreplay is vital," she adds nonchalantly while I melt into a lust puddle.

"Jesus, Sunshine. You're killing me. When did you get so bold?" My palm slams on the table behind her to steady my buckling knees. "I might actually blow," I admit before inhaling her sweet coconut scent. She always smells like the beach, or at least how I imagine it.

"You bring out a naughty side of me, Ryker," she murmurs as her fingers dance up my ribs.

I swallow loudly, trying to hold back. "Sunshine," I warn quietly while staring into her heated gaze.

She purrs against my jaw, "What's your fantasy?"

"You."

"What about me? Anything special?"

"Everything. You're the entire package, all I could want and need. You're really special for me," I admit without thought.

Flush races up the column of her throat before settling into her pink cheeks. My chest puffs up in honor—I caused that reaction.

Lennon hums and the soft exhale whisks across my stubbled jaw.

"You're so sweet, Ryker. Wanna know mine?"

"God, yes," I beg and rock into her.

My eyes cross as I imagine the possibilities.

"You watching me, staring openly while I slowly get undressed. You're peering through the window as I begin touching myself to thoughts of your blazing blue gaze taking the scene in. When I tumble over the edge, wishing it was your hand, you'll be pleading for release too," Lennon's voice trembles while exposing her secret desires.

"Shit."

Her words are so much better than I could have anticipated. Does she know how often I've pictured this exact scenario?

"Maybe we could act that out sometime?" I ask around the arousal threatening to choke me.

"I would really like that."

"Do you want me to touch you now?" I offer hesitantly.

Lennon giggles.

"Not here, but tonight . . ." When she beams at me, a lopsided grin lifts my lips. "Pretty sure we're not getting anything else done. Time to go?"

"But I thought we were going to the—"

"Wouldn't that be a perfect spot for further *exploration*?" She accentuates the word and I get dizzy from the lack of blood flow to my brain.

My tongue swells so all I can do is signal her to lead the way.

As we're about to leave the studio, Lennon's phone pings and she stops in her tracks after glancing at the screen.

"Holy shit!" she exclaims while continuing to read the message.

"What it is, Sunshine? Is everything alright?"

Lennon looks at me and her eyes are glassy with unshed tears.

"Guess what?"

"Just tell me."

"I won," she squeals. "I got first place in the logo content."

My face splits into a wide smile as I yank her toward me. Lennon bounces in my hold so I hoist her into my arms before spinning us round and round. She laughs loudly and I follow suit, glad to be sharing this moment with her. Lennon tosses her head back with another buoyant giggle before clasping her hands on my cheeks.

"I can't believe this. That prize money gives Len's Looks a real chance."

"I'm not at all surprised, Sunshine. That design was brilliant, like everything else you make."

"We need to celebrate," she states as her eyes shine bright.

"Tequila?"

Her face goes a little green as the word leaves my lips.

"I just threw up in my mouth a little bit. Pretty sure champagne would be better."

"Good call. Let's stop on the way."

"This night is gonna be one to remember," she says and wags her brow.

A sharp groan escapes as I start walking out. Lennon is still wrapped around me, exactly where she should be. I'd carry her everywhere if she'd let me.

"I have no doubt about that, Sunshine."

"I can hardly wait," she whispers in my ear.

With temptation personified seated next to me, the drive seems cut in half. I should be more careful with precious cargo but the possibility of touching Lennon's smooth skin is making me reckless. We haven't spoken a word the entire ride as friction crackles around us. I almost pull over several times but she's looking forward to crossing this first off our list.

Right at dusk, we pull into the dusty lot and I park in the back along the edge. The drive-in theater should be fantastic but for far different reasons than I'd imagined. As I kill the engine, restless energy skitters along my flesh, sitting still isn't an option. I get to work unloading the blankets and pillows before setting up a makeshift mattress in the bed of my truck.

Lennon rests against the lowered tailgate. "Are you all right? Your pace is like . . . triple the usual."

"Yep, all good. Just really excited for this," I ramble while tossing the final layer down.

"I had no idea you enjoyed the art of cinematography so much." She tips forward, laughter shaking her shoulders.

When I turn to face her the sun has almost set and she glows in the dim light.

"Uh," I stammer. Is Lennon actually expecting to watch these movies? *Shit.* "What's playing again?"

This time she bends backward in full on cackles.

"Your face," she wheezes. "Oh my God, Ryker. You're looking at me like I just ruined Christmas. Don't worry, Santa really does exist." Humor bounces on her tone.

"Get your butt up here and we'll see who's laughing."

"What are you gonna do? Give me a spanking?" She nibbles on her lip before winking at me.

It's my turn to double over, but not from laughter. If I don't lose the visual of her creamy ass beneath my palm, this will be over before it begins. My legs give out from the strain and I topple onto the puffy comforter.

"Sunshine," I moan to the dark sky and press down on my aching junk. "What am I going to do with you? My balls are never going to recover."

Suddenly her beautiful face is hovering above me, lighting up the black scenery.

"What's wrong with them?" She peeks at my cupped hand before swinging her eyes back to me. "Are you hurt?" An adorable crease forms between her brows.

The pressure eases with her concern but the dirty desires shove to the front of my mind. "I'm fine," I huff between my clenched teeth. "Lay down with me. The show is about to start."

Lennon's head nestles on my pec while I adjust higher on the mountain of cushions, propping us up in case we watch the movie. Her palm rests against my flexed abs and I try to ignore the potent desire barreling through me. If we act on our lustful urges, Lennon needs to make the first move. My racing heart demands certainty before giving into my filthy fantasies.

I try to get comfortable and relax my straining muscles but it's impossible with her fingers toying at the hem of my shirt. The hand resting against her hip squeezes into a fist when her nails drag lightly against the taut skin of my lower stomach. I blow out a deep breath and beg for patience as the enormous screen flickers to life in front of us.

When the opening credits begin rolling, Lennon's warm breath tickles my neck before she places a delicate kiss there. She decadently drops lingering pecks up toward my ear and my vision gets hazy. When her lips suck along my jaw and her entire palm slides up my abdomen, I'm ready to bust. My fingers find the edge of her top before brushing her silky skin. Lennon shivers as she reaches my mouth so I haul her closer and fuse us together.

As our lips connect, I roll onto my side and pull her so our bodies are better aligned. I groan into her open mouth and she responds by stroking my tongue with hers. I devour her sweet flavor while both hands tremble with need, my deeper cravings begging for satisfaction.

"Can I touch you?" I plead between sinful kisses.

Lennon nods vigorously before diving back into my mouth. My palm traces up her spine before finding the clasp of her bra. My inexperienced fingers fumble with the hook and my face heats with the lack of skill. Lennon reaches and expertly snaps the strap open before returning to her delicate exploration of my torso. I don't dwell or doddle as my hungry hand fills with her naked flesh. My touch glides between her plump tits. Lennon wriggles against me and mews against my lips when I rub her peaked nipple. My fingers focus there, playing with the hardened point and rounding the tightened skin before pinching slightly.

"Yes," she breathes quietly. "More, *please*."

I eagerly follow her request, alternating soft flicks with gentle tweaks, lavishing her pebbled tips with undivided attention. My mouth waters for a taste but removing the obtrusive fabric isn't an option even if it's dark and secluded.

Lennon breaks away and pants, "I want things but don't know how to ask for them."

"Tell me," I beg. "I'll give you anything."

"Here," she says while dragging my hand down to her waist. "Touch me there." Her hips bump into me, giving further permission and arousal shoots through my veins.

I suck in sharply and try to cool the need taking over my body. I'm already on edge, ready to blow, and haven't made this good enough for her yet. Tremors cause my fingers to be extra clumsy while attempting to unbutton her jeans and I curse my inexperience. Why couldn't she be wearing a dress like usual?

Lennon stills my awkward movements with her steady hand.

"Don't be nervous. I've never done this before either. Just go slow, okay?" She whispers against my slack jaw.

I blindly reach behind me for a discarded blanket and throw it over us before successfully opening the closure.

I freeze, uncertainty chilling my bones, and my fingers stall on the zipper. "I don't want to hurt you." The words tumble out without warning, my frazzled brain short circuiting with this overwhelming onslaught.

"You won't," Lennon reassures before shimming the denim down her hips. She guides my suddenly stiff digits to the elastic waistband of her panties. "You'll only bring me pleasure. I'll show you."

Our entwined fingers move under the cotton and she pushes my hand farther down, along bare skin and into velvet slickness, until her heated center is beneath my fingertips. A gasp escapes at the raw feeling.

"You're wet," I murmur as wonder pours from me and I stare down at her with wide eyes.

"You really turn me on," she explains as her lashes flutter.

My pulse soars.

"I do?"

Lennon nods while rocking into me. "Yes, so much." Her back bends so her core settles deeper against me. "Right here," she instructs while circling my finger over a small bump.

Even though I can't see what's happening under the blanket, the other sensations tell me enough. Lennon grows wetter as I spin around that special spot and quiet cries spill from her throat. My dick jerks and pulses behind the zipper but I ignore the ferocious lust.

My fingers work faster with Lennon's commands of more and harder. Her nails bite into my arm as she bows up, her light gaze stabs into me before those aqua eyes roll back into her head. The soft noises drip from her tongue like a siren call demanding to be answered, and I eagerly offer more rapid strokes. I'm riveted to the ecstasy flashing over her features, the expression clear and beautiful to watch. She steals the show.

"I'm going to come," she gasps.

"Me too," I echo against her throat.

Lennon quivers and vibrates against me as she whispers her pleasure into my throat. My fingers are coated with her pure essence as I keep stroking her. Any remaining control vanishes and she triggers my release, liquid fire pooling in my gut before blasting from me, and I'm powerless to stop it. My body shudders and trembles along hers as we float into the weightless atmosphere.

With labored exhales and aftershocks twitching our limbs, we return to the surface, clutching onto each other with all our might.

"Wow, that was so much better than when I do it." Lennon blinks at me and something sparkles in her turquoise stare. "I can't believe that's the first thing to pop out of my mouth," she mutters before hiding her flaming face behind her hands.

I pry her shield away as a rumble shakes my chest.

"Never hide from me, even if you're embarrassed. You make me laugh with your unfiltered thoughts." I press a chaste kiss to her lips. "Thank you for giving me that. Watching you come from my touch is a precious treasure. Another thing I'm not deserving of but will graciously accept. You're a dream, Sunshine. I can't believe this is real."

She sniffles and swallows loudly. "How could I possibly cry after getting the best orgasm ever?" Lennon shakes her head before reaching for me. "I'm so selfish. It's your turn."

My hips jump away to evade her touch, fearful she'll feel the sticky mess I've made in my briefs.

"I already did." Heat races up my throat with the confession.

"But I didn't get to touch you," she pouts and I kiss her puffy.

"You didn't have to. Touching you and watching you fall apart in my arms was more than enough."

Lennon sighs and her gaze skitters to the side.

"Well, can you go again? They do in the movies. I mean, so, we can . . . you know?" She asks and points between us.

"Now? Here?" I sputter in surprise.

She nods eagerly and grips the buckle of my belt. I rest my hand over hers, halting the hasty movements.

"Can we be open and honest right now?"

"Always, please and thank you."

"Will you tell me how you want our first time to be? For real?" My heart and soul refuse to take her for the first time in the back of my truck.

"I want you. That's it." Lennon's nails scratch up my abs, getting me hard again, as she keeps talking. "I don't need a fancy hotel room or a big extravagant plan. I just want with be with you, in the most organic way possible. Just like nature intended. We don't need to make this complicated or overthink things. We can just . . . let it happen," She trails off, scanning my tense features.

"I overthink everything, Lennon." Worry works its way into my system. If I refuse her, will she get upset? "I'm glad you're not particularly fussy but we've gotta do better than this." My mind flips through readily available options and an idea solidifies in my dazed mind. "Let's go to my place."

"As in your apartment? You've never brought me there before." Lennon seems startled by my suggestion.

"I wasn't keeping it from you or anything," I mutter and shrug. "There's nothing really exciting about it." My heart hammers erratically, imagining her reaction.

"And you want to bring me there, rather than have me here, because . . ." Her curiosity trails off, as if waiting for me to finish her thought.

"You'll see, Sunshine."

nineteen

LENNON

The answer will always be you.

RYKER UNLOCKS THE DOOR BEFORE stepping aside, allowing me to enter first. The room appears to be empty but it's hard to be certain in the dark. As he flips a switch, the space is flooded with light and my suspicions are correct. I scour the area, looking for anything of meaning, something that represents the amazing guy behind me. The blank white walls and barren wood floors are depressing.

This is where he lives?

My body has been keyed up since Ryker blew my effing mind with that orgasm but now I'm toppling back to reality. Over the last several weeks, I've managed to forget how alone Ryker was before we started dating. This is a stark reminder I wasn't prepared for, and it's really upsetting.

"How can you . . . I mean, did you just move in? Or have you already started packing for Denten?" My hopeful heart searches for boxes stacked in the corners but of course, I find none. A spasm attacks my stomach, picturing this sweet man alone in this bleak existence.

Ryker's hands burrow deep in his pockets as he shrugs. "I know it doesn't look like much, mostly because it isn't, but it serves a purpose. This place is nothing more than a spot to rest my head."

My brow raises skeptically while glancing at him.

"Uh, all right." I shuffle into the kitchen before opening the fridge. Nothing. Freezer? Bare. "So, you stay here but don't really live here? A house but not a home?"

"Yeah, that's about it. Not like I'm entertaining often or have anything worth displaying." His tone is low and flat. "Can you hang out a sec? Just gotta change my pants."

I nod mutely while wondering why the hell he needs to switch clothes. My focus doesn't linger long after he disappears from sight. I wander into the living room where a desk, laptop, several monitors, and an office chair are pushed against the wall. Besides the electronics, this space is vacant too. Chills creep under my skin and I rub my arms briskly to ward off the eerie feeling.

My gaze skitters down the hallway in the direction Ryker went. A lump forms in my throat as I picture his bedroom, his most personal space, void of any warmth just like the rest. Desperation to provide comfort pushes me forward. Nervous energy rattles through my chest as I move closer.

Ryker appears, as if hearing my thoughts, and all sadness washes away as my eyes land on him. My mouth waters at the first glimpse of this sexy guy wearing nothing but a pair of light gray sweats. What is it about men and baggy sweatpants? Scratch that. Not just any man—*Ryker*. I must have been very good in my previous life to deserve him. And he's all mine.

Pretty sure I'm drooling.

I wipe at my lips to make sure. His upper body is on display, and my vision is full of lightly bronzed skin and rippling muscles. Ryker's bare shoulders are sculped stacks of power that roll back as he walks toward me. His torso is lined with deep ridges that lead down to the tantalizing V of his hips. He's cut and chiseled *everywhere* my starving eyes can see. My fingers want to feel every glorious inch and I'm not ashamed of staring. Ryker wouldn't come out here barely clothed if he didn't want me to gawk.

Good Lord, he's perfection.

My surroundings no longer matter and heat unfurls from my core. Who cares about his choices in decorating, or lack thereof? In two short weeks, we'll be outta here and can decorate our new studio together. Forget all that mopey stuff because I have one important goal now.

Getting naked.

"Y-you lo-look," I stutter before blurting, "fucking hot." My chin dips as I groan loudly, wishing for an invisibility cloak. Can't I be the least bit seductive?

I peek up at Mr. Sexy Pants and find a dimpled smirk quirking his sinful lips. Everything inside of me turns to goo when I realize it doesn't matter what comes out of my mouth. Ryker gets me.

"Lemme show you something, Sunshine." He reaches for me.

Hopefully that involves the enormous package saluting me from below his waist. I might be a virgin but it's *very* obvious what's about to happen. Our fingers lace effortlessly and the familiar buzz prickles up my arm. Ryker leads me to a closed door then tugs me in front of him so I'm perfectly notched against the impressive bulge in his pants.

"Close your eyes," he whispers while gripping the knob in front of us.

I comply and after a soft *whoosh*, Ryker guides me forward with his hands on my hips. His hold tightens as he murmurs, "Now open."

My lids shutter rapidly against the unexpected light while I adjust to the glowing hues scattered around the space. A tremendous wave crashes into me and I wobble in place from the sudden dizziness.

Before me is the most beautiful room I could ever image. It's impossible to settle my sight on any one thing. My eyes bounce wildly around the brightly colored room for a few moments, silently absorbing each piece.

The enormous bed sits in the middle, covered in sunny yellow sheets. The pillows look fluffy and soft, exactly how I like them. There's a kitschy dresser and nightstand set that looks very similar to a combo I've had my eye on. The teal color pops against the lighter shades. Most of all though, I'm stunned by the pseudo wallpaper.

"Oh my . . . Wh-what is all this?" My voice wavers as I continue digesting the glorious space. My fingers brush one of the little yellow notes stuck to the wall.

When you tip your head to the sky, it's like you're saying hello to an old friend.

My gaze bounces across a few more that paint the space.

Hello, Beautiful.

You make my life better just by existing.

Favorite #54: the way your eyes crinkle at the corners when you laugh.

Everything I am is because of you.

Every available inch is covered with sunny squares for rows and rows, arranged all about, no real rhyme or reason or pattern. My mind overloads as my vision blurs, but the message remains clear.

Ryker clears his throat and I twist slightly to face him.

"I guess," he scratches his flushed nape, "it seems pretty strange to have a room like this, made up for you, just in case."

His speech fumbles as he glances around, but all I see in this moment is him. Ryker's bare chest expands with a heavy breath. "This was another way of keeping you nearby. I'd picture you in here, working on homework or sewing or writing or . . . *whatever.* When I was extra lonely because you were busy next door, I'd write a few notes for your space here." His ocean irises blast into me and I swear he reaches my soul.

"Wow." I read a couple more notes before getting lost in him again. "This is the most romantic thing I've ever seen. Instead of rose petals scattered on the mattress and floor, you've flooded the wall with words of endearment."

"Of love," Ryker interjects.

My heart leaps into my throat.

"What?"

"These are my words of love to you."

"What are you saying, Ryker?" A few tears track down my heated cheeks as I stare up at this beautiful man.

His thumb swipes away the drops.

"I love you, Sunshine." He peels off a note and hands it to me. "See?"

"I don't expect you to say it back," Ryker continues seamlessly. "I've never been cared for. The fact you tolerate my presence, let alone want and like me, is beyond any expectation. Please don't feel—"

Before another word escapes his gracious mouth, I leap into his arms without warning. I capture his handsome face between my palms as he yanks me closer.

"Stop selling yourself short. Never again. I love you, Ryker." I kiss his parted lips. "Of course, I love you. How could I not?"

His eyes shine with emotion before he nuzzles into my neck.

"You love me," he repeats but doesn't question. He believes my words just as intended.

Without another syllable, my legs wind around him and Ryker hikes me higher with his hands cradling my ass. He carries me to the perfectly made bed covered in sunny yellow sheets, which appears brand new and never touched. As he lays us down, I ask if this is where he usually sleeps.

Ryker shakes his head while brushing stray strands from my face.

"No. This space is yours, or ours now I suppose."

The fabric is silky and heavenly underneath me but my attention remains on the man propped above me. "This is exactly where we're meant to be. Right here," I breathe against his jaw as my fingers skate down, tracing along the muscular grooves in his back. This room was created with love and it's fitting that I'll worship him here.

"Are you sure?" he asks.

"Yes," I sigh before sealing our lips together.

My hips lift into his as I pull him further down, successfully grinding us together. Ryker's hands fidget with the hem of my shirt until I arch for him to drag it up and off. I find his mouth again as he reaches to undo my bra. As the bare flesh of our chests touch for the first time, something foreign wakes up inside of me. My skin is hyperaware as tentative touches are exchanged.

His rough palms glide up my sides and my nipples pebble tight, pressing against his stony pecs.

Ryker rises up, his focus on my jeans.

"I want you naked," he utters into the silence.

I rock into his trembling hands, letting him know I need that too. Denim and cotton slide down my quaking thighs and Ryker's blue irises feast on each newly exposed piece of me. He stands to remove his pants before his body blankets mine, both of us free from material restraints. His hardness rests against my soft belly as Ryker begins cherishing me with his mouth. Starting with a kiss to my taut throat then trailing down my fluttering pulse. His lips latch onto my sensitive breasts before kissing along my stomach, goosebumps rising with his descent. When he settles between my legs, I suck in an anxious breath before spreading wider in anticipation.

His lips and fingers make love to the most innocent part of me, preparing my body for more with the utmost care. I soon discover new heights from Ryker's generous and devoted affections. My toes curl as sparks zap up my calves and warmth spreads rapidly from my core. His hands stroke under my bare thighs, skimming along my ass, before drifting up against the smooth skin of my back. Ryker's thumbs play along my ribs, the bumps and dips providing contrasting sensations, each bone providing a new tune.

"You're so beautiful, Sunshine." Ryker's voice rumbles from deep within.

His heated stare roams up my exposed body like a silky caress. He studies me like an artist, ready to shape and mold my bland existence into something breathtaking. I want his mark all over my body, like the one he's already branded into my soul, a special signature meant only for me.

I reach for him, ready to feel his velvety steel in my palm, but Ryker has other plans. He brings both of my wrists to his lips, pressing barely-there kisses along the delicate skin, before placing my palms on his biceps. Ryker lowers down very slowly, his arms shaking from the strain. When his tense face hovers over mine, I realize he's trembling everywhere. My fingertips dance down his spine before sweeping back up to grip his shoulders.

He groans out a choppy exhale.

"Holy shit, that feels so good."

"I want to give you something even better," I promise before squirming beneath him.

My knees lift around his hips and I draw him in closer, silently asking for what my body is craving without uttering a word. Ryker sucks in a jagged breath before adjusting our connection, searching for what we both desire. His frantic eyes lock on me, the blue waves violent and crashing wildly deep inside him. When I feel him *there*, hard and ready, my heart pounds feverishly as wildfire roars through my veins. My head bobs wildly before yanking his mouth to mine.

I choke on a harsh breath as the initial stab of pain slices into me and Ryker freezes in place, muscles locked up tight. He breaks away from my lips, the intention to stop altogether reflecting in his eyes.

"It's okay, keep going. *Please.* I'm okay," I reassure him while shifting slightly to ease the radiating ache.

Ryker doesn't appear convinced and remains still. "I never want to hurt you."

"I know. Trust me," I offer through a wobbly grin. "Our first time isn't meant to be flawless but this is far more than just sex. This is the final barrier between us, a wall taken down so we can truly be whole together. Now we're joined as one," I murmur against his mouth before sucking on his bottom lip. "We have forever to make perfect love, but this is the only moment we'll have our first time." I nod slowly and after a beat, he mimics the movement.

A deep crease forms between Ryker's dark brows as he presses his mouth back to mine and pushes further into me. As I welcome him into my body, everything I am becomes his. The movements aren't effortless or easy but that makes it ours. We've been waiting our entire lives to share this raw experience and chose each other. That's worth the discomfort pulsing through me. This is how we're meant to connect our bodies together for the very first time.

We take our time, there's no rush. As he discovers and explores the plains of my flesh, he plants delicate touches to his favorite spots. A gentle graze of teeth to my collarbone. A rasp of scruff along my cleavage. An exquisite path of kisses up my neck. Sweat collects on our brows as we rock together in unison. Each move is slow and calculated for maximum impact. He slides in and I arch against him, tightening my hold everywhere. As he glides out, I grip him harder, refusing to let go. Ryker trembles on top of me and tells me he can't hold back much longer.

"It's okay. Give me your love," I whisper.

He does with a loud groan into my mouth as spasms pop through his joints. I cuddle him closer, gaining pleasure from his ecstasy, until he's wrung out.

Ryker's breathing is labored as he props up on his elbows. His sapphire eyes are bright with wonder and astonishment colors his tone.

"I've dreamed of this countless times, experiencing this with you, but I never dared to . . ." His words taper off as he scans my features.

My nails lightly scratch along his buzzed scalp and he shivers against me. "Tell me," I urge when he stays silent.

"I didn't allow myself to really hope it could ever happen. You've made my unbelievable fantasy come true." He worries his bottom lip before adding, "And next time I'll make it better for you."

I kiss his concern away.

"This has been the best day in paradise. Being that close to you was the greatest thing. Never doubt your ability to make me happy," I say while cupping his blotchy cheek.

Ryker leans into my touch before dusting my mouth with a sweet kiss.

"I'm so damn lucky, Sunshine. You're my every wish." He rolls off me and reaches above our heads. When he settles next to me, a yellow note is in his hand. "This always seemed impossible but that didn't stop me from writing it."

I hope you'll sleep here one day, surrounded by sunlight and love.

The bold script distorts as my eyes mist over. I snuggle into his warm embrace, my bare skin melting into his, and vibrant intimacy hums around us.

"You're really something, Ryker. I'm so thankful for you."

He hugs me closer and nothing has ever felt so right. Not college or my designs or the potential of having a successful business. Suddenly I remember something.

"Ryker?" I question softly into the comfortable quiet.

"Hmm?" He murmurs against my temple.

"What's your first favorite thing? I saw number fifty-four on the wall."

I feel his lips quirk along my skin.

"Ah, that's easy. Your smile."

My response is exactly that, a huge toothy grin that stretches my entire face. I can't help the giddy glee spreading through me.

"Yeah, that's the one," he whispers softly into my ear.

Suddenly Ryker rises from the bed and I instantly miss his warmth. He disappears into the bathroom for a few moments before returning with a washcloth. Emotion lodges in my throat at his tenderness as he settles in next to me. Ryker takes great care cleaning me up and I arch closer with each tentative touch.

After tossing the cloth away, he draws me into his body so we're cuddling without any space separating us.

I drift off to sleep with visions of the crystal-clear ocean lapping gently along the sandy shore, joining as one for all of eternity.

twenty
RYKER

I want you, only you.
I don't care about anything else.

MY EYES RAPIDLY SCAN THE computer screen but are beginning to feel heavy. Instead of sleeping, I've been logging yesterday's data and adding to my latest software update. Lennon stirs next to me, rolling onto her back and stretching languidly like a lazy cat on a Sunday afternoon. A high-pitched, drawn out noise shatters the silence as she yawns while bending her spine further. Her lashes flutter open slowly, gracing me with stunning aqua gems that beckon me closer with a simple look.

Watching Lennon wake up is a glorious sight.

"Good morning, Ry." Her voice is a drowsy rasp, coated with sand and grit.

"Ry? Haven't heard that one yet." My lips tip up automatically, my smile becoming familiar.

"Uh huh," mumbles out from behind her fingers as she snuggles under the covers. "It just flew back into my foggy mind. Seems fitting to call you something special after our first co-ed slumber party." Lennon smirks and my heart tumbles a little farther.

I snap the laptop shut before setting it aside, the string of code in front of me no longer holding any interest. My hands easily scoop up her tiny frame and draw her onto me.

"I can't wait to enjoy this sleeping arrangement from now on. Speaking of, are you ready to tell me where we're going on this secret trip yet? I wanna know where you're taking me."

"Nope," she replies with extra pop to the p.

"Come on, Sunshine. I need to know what to pack."

"I've already told you we're going camping. That's all you're getting out of me."

"But I've never done that sort of thing before. If you'll be more specific, that'll make it easier for me. Spill the details," I say while dropping my lips to hers.

Lennon yelps and tries pulling away but my arms band tight around her.

"I have morning breath! I need to brush my teeth before we do any of that," she squeals while struggling in my hold.

"Never deny me," I murmur before stealing a kiss regardless.

Lennon melts against me, the fight leaving her almost immediately. After satisfying my need for her taste, I break away and blindly reach for her breakfast behind me.

Her eyes widen as they catch sight of what's in my grasp.

"Gah, you're the absolute best. Coffee with a bagel and Ry in bed? All of my favorites before," she glances at the nightstand, "eight o'clock? Maybe you should pinch me because I might be dreaming." Lennon giggles as I nibble up her neck, proving she's very much awake.

We break apart and she glides up against the headboard, tucking the sheet carefully under her arms before making quick work of unwrapping the food. The seemingly unconscious actions are fluid and full of pose, just like everything about her. After a huge bite, she moans while chewing. Lennon gulps a hearty swallow of hazelnut java before beaming at me.

"It's official, you're spoiling me. A girl can definitely get used to all this."

Pride swells in my chest.

"Good. Your happiness means I've done my job well."

"Did you already eat?" Lennon hums while chewing. Wait," her gaze swings to me. "You left to pick this up?"

I grunt at the ridiculous notion.

"Hell no. I wouldn't miss a moment of you wrapped in my arms and resting soundly after being worn out." My face burns with the memory of her naked flesh against mine. I shake the image away before my body demands another round. "The cafe delivers for me."

"They do? How am I just learning this now?" Lennon's nose wrinkles.

"Uh," I stumble over the explanation. "If you pay enough, they'll do it without question."

"How much money do you make exactly? If you don't mind me asking." She takes a sip as her head tilts slightly.

"I stopped keeping track but plenty. Enough to never have to worry, that's for sure" I answer without hesitation.

"Wow. I can't fathom having that type of financial security."

"Well, you should. It's all for you, Sunshine."

"Oh, no. Not this again." Her dark hair whips all about. "I gave in about the studio rent but that doesn't mean you're paying for everything. I'm capable of taking care of stuff too. Especially after winning that logo contest." Her aqua gaze glows as a matching grin splits her lips.

I entwine our fingers and squeeze gently.

"I'm so damn proud of you, Sunshine. That award was yours from the start," I say before brushing a soft peck to her forehead. "And I'd never stop you from doing anything. Well, except leave me."

Lennon scoffs at my amendment.

"I have more than enough for us to use however we like. If you'd like to chip in, I won't refuse but it would be better to spend what you have on Len's Looks. I'm more than willing to invest in your company too, if you'd let me. I want to provide everything so you can rely on me."

"All that sweet talk sounds very good coming from you," Lennon says before brushing a brisk kiss to my jaw. "But what about your goals and personal achievements? Cost of living?"

"You saw my apartment." My thumb hikes to the hallway. "Aside from this room, I live a very minimalist lifestyle. I always have and that's fine. I want more for us, together. If I have it, we should use it." I squeeze her leg and tap the computer before adding, "My accomplishments are all right here. This space I created for us isn't too bad, right? I've built a few very lucrative software programs by the age of twenty-two. That was a pretty damn good start. Now? I've got you." I pull her palm to my lips. "I don't need anything else ever again."

"Well, alrighty then." Lennon sniffles a bit.

"Alrighty then," I echo with a small smile.

Her fingers graze underneath my eyes. "Did you sleep all right? There's purple smudges here."

"Nah," I respond with a sheepish shrug. "My nights are always busy. I work out to quiet my anxiety before getting work done. I've never needed more than a few hours. That's just the way it is."

"Is there anything I can do to help? I want you to find peace and be able to relax." Lennon's brow crinkles.

"Oh, you do plenty. Without you here, I'd be a complete disaster. You bring a level of calm to my life that I can't achieve alone. Not even a little bit, trust me." I smooth the worry from her skin with my thumb. "Because of you, I've actually been sleeping more than usual but didn't catch a wink last night for obvious reasons."

A brilliant blush bursts across her cheeks and all I can do is watch, totally enraptured, while my words cause such an impact. Her reaction reminds me of all that lies ahead for us.

"Where to next, Sunshine?" I ask after a few silent moments.

"What do you mean? We can't stay in here forever, surrounded by love notes?" She looks around the room with raw emotion shining in her eyes.

"Does that include staying naked? Because I'm totally game. We could start with a shower," I mumble against her bare shoulder.

"Together?" she squeaks sharply, and a blush races up her neck as she yanks the blanket higher.

"Why are you hiding from me? We shared everything last night," I ask and drag my finger under the offensive fabric. I tug lightly against the dip between her tits. "There's no need to be shy, Sunshine."

"Easy for you to say, Mister Sexy Pants." Lennon raises an angular brow.

My burst of laughter is loud and unexpected.

"Another nickname? I won't even ask." I stare deeply into her light eyes and my gut dips at the open affection reflected back at me. "You're gorgeous. Never doubt that. It should be glaringly obvious that I'm legit crazy over you, Missus Sexy Pants." I can't stop the words from tumbling out and she shivers against me.

"Missus?" Lennon questions softly while looking up through lowered lashes.

"That just slipped out but I don't take it back. That title sounds right."

"It really does."

"You're my future, Sunshine. I'd do anything for you, which includes hours of worship and special attention."

"Really?"

"Need me to show you?"

She nods rapidly and that's all I need to be set in motion. My greedy hands grip her hips before she's hoisted into my arms. As I'm carrying her into the bathroom, my mouth waters at the expanse of creamy skin on full display.

"I'm gonna love all over you and make up for the pain last night. This is all about you," I whisper and watch goosebumps rise along her flesh.

With the warm water cascading down around us, I kiss and suck and lick every succulent piece of her until Lennon is a rippling puddle in my palms. I don't consider my own release even when my cock begs for relief, knowing she's probably sore. Roaring arousal pumps through me regardless, proving I don't need to get off for this to feel good. Lennon pouts and reaches for my painfully hard length, demanding to return the favor. I shake my head and latch onto her mouth, silencing any further protest.

A relaxed smile lifts her lips as I take my time washing her pliable form, making sure to massage the soap into her sluggish muscles. The small space smells like coconut and the beach and paradise, which is exactly why I bought a bottle of her shampoo. Getting clean has never been so dirty and doesn't last nearly long enough in my opinion, but Lennon's fingertips are starting to prune. I take my time toweling her off, enjoying the feel of her curves underneath the soft terry cloth.

We get out and wander into the bedroom. I step into a pair of sweats before grabbing a shirt for her. It's far too large but Lennon doesn't complain as she slips it on. Her sinful body is covered from my hungry gaze but I'll never leave her alone if she stays naked. A pleased grumble barrels from my chest as the fabric brushes her knees. Having Lennon wear my clothes is a fucking nice alternative to seeing her bare.

"Thanks. For, uh, everything. How the heck did you get so good at, um, all that sexy stuff?" She shoots me a shy smile and fidgets with the hem. A rosy hue blossoms across her features and I know it's not from the clammy air clinging around us.

"You want the honest truth?" Shame paints the words and worry slithers up my torso. Lennon nods while stepping closer to me, a frown denting her forehead. I blow out heavy sigh. "I did a lot of research in preparation. Like advice columns, articles, chat rooms, and . . . uh, porn." I choke out the last part. Lennon stares at me silently, no reaction whatsoever. My blood pressure spikes, assuming the worst. *Shit.* "It's not like I was doing it for pleasure or anything. Don't be mad. I didn't enjoy watching them," I tell her honestly.

Lennon chews on her lip before a giggle bubbles out. "Why would I be mad? Don't guys watch dirty videos all the time? I mean, kudos to whatever you studied, it worked *really* well." The statement comes across as a fact, not her padding my ego. She bites her lip before adding, "I really like what you do. Now I feel bad for not doing anything to make it better for you. Urgh, I totally suck."

"Not possible," I assure her as I loop my arms around her waist. "You'll always—"

"Let's watch some together," Lennon blurts while fiddling with the drawstring on my pants.

"Now? You're serious?" I sputter.

"Yeah, why not?" She shrugs. "It'll give us something to do while we finish cooling off."

"Um, that kind of defeats the purpose of watching it," I utter and my dick stirs at her fingers' close proximity.

"No. This is for instructional use only." She shakes her finger at me. "I want some pointers before we head out of town later. This camping trip will be super romantic *and* sexy now." Her blue-green eyes sparkle in the low light. "Plus, I still need to pack and can't spend all day in bed. No matter how hot and bothered these pornos make me."

An amused huff puffs from my mouth before I lead us to the bed. I grab my laptop before opening a free site I'd found during my exploration.

"These aren't that great so don't expect much. I learned more from the blog posts," I offer softly while clicking through all the permission tabs.

"Oh, hush. It's only fair. Lucy always talked about watching this sort of thing but I never saw the point. If nothing else, it will be another first for me," she says and reaches for my hand.

Suddenly lude noises blast from the tiny speakers. Filthy language and corny moans fill the quiet room as we sit extremely still, watching the small screen. Our heads tilt toward each other, trying to figure out the unnatural position. My stomach flips and awkwardness creeps up my spine. This entire situation doesn't feel right—at all.

"Oh my. Wow." Lennon's eyes bulge. "Um, okay. That's . . . interesting." She gestures at the computer. "How does she bend like that? That can't be comfortable. Isn't there a 101-beginner's version?"

"See? I warned you. Totally over the top and not very helpful." I click out of the video before tossing the laptop aside.

She starts laughing.

"I'm not even sure what to call that. I might be scarred for life." She pats her temple before fanning her face. "Phew, well that's done. Should we get ready to go?" Lennon twists and kisses my cheek before hopping off the springy mattress.

"Are you going to tell me where yet? Or still keeping it a secret?" I question as Lennon bounces in front of me. She insisted on planning this next date on her own, only sharing that we'd be gone for several days and that it involved a tent. Apparently, my sunshine isn't into glamping, whatever that means.

She laces our fingers and tugs me off the bed. "It's going to be so much fun. You'll see. Come on, come on. There's a dive restaurant on the way that we can check out for lunch. How much time do you need to get ready?" Lennon talks at rapid speed and my ears buzz while attempting to intake everything.

I rub her palm over my cropped hair.

"Ready when you are, Sexy Pants."

twenty-one
LENNON

I STEP BACK BEFORE WIPING my damp brow, pride filling my chest at our teamwork. My lungs expel a long exhale as I stretch the strain in my lower back. Setting up a tent is no joke but the effort was well worth it.

After securing the final stake, Ryker stands to join me and we take a moment to admire our rustic setup. The section of shaded grass we're renting is completely surrounded by natural beauty. Dense trees line most of the space except for the section of sandy shore. The rocky cliffs rise up in the distance and edge the far side of the lake. I can hear the crashing rush of the waterfall just around the bend but it's hidden from view. The sun reflects through the leaves and casts shimmering light around the small space. This slice of wilderness is our home for the next several days and the tranquil scenery is practically humming with peace.

The campsites at Clifftop Outpost are secluded and widely spread apart for privacy. Their promise of a quiet escape from city living caught my attention when I was planning this surprise for us. I'd say they definitely held up their end of the bargain.

My lids blink quickly as I twist to peer at the calm lake. The surface glistens as slow waves ripple with the breeze, beckoning us near. This oppressive June humidity has me craving a swim in the cool water. I tip my face up to Ryker and catch him staring at me.

"Whatcha looking at?" I question with a smirk.

"You," he says without pause.

"Why?"

He shrugs and reaches for my hand. "Because that's kinda my thing. It's what I do. What I've done for years. Do you want me to stop?" Ryker's eyes spear into me and my knees threaten to buckle.

"No. I um, like it. *A lot.*" I stress the last word and bite my lip.

"Good," he hums while tucking me into his side, "because I wasn't going to quit."

I hop on tiptoes and tip my face toward his.

"I love you, Ry."

Even with the sweltering heat blasting against us, Ryker shivers.

"I love hearing that from your lips. Almost as much as I love you, Sunshine." His prickly jaw nuzzles along my sticky cheek and even with the balmy weather, I welcome the embrace.

"This place is all right, huh? Not too shabby?"

Ryker guffaws. "You're joking, right? Because you did real good. This spot is dynamite and has everything we need." He gestures around us and I follow the sweep of his arm. "It'll be fun to have a fire later. We can snuggle close for warmth."

When he wags his brows, I giggle into his shoulder.

"Oh, I like the sound of that." My lashes bat shamelessly up at him.

Ryker chuckles again and the sound brings flutters to my belly.

"I love you but there's no way we're gettin' busy in that tent right now. It's too fucking hot, but I'll show you later."

I gawk unabashedly at his open expression.

Oh, my. Playful and flirty Ryker is hazardous to my lady bits.

"What?" He questions after I keep silently staring.

"You're so . . . *sexy*," I blurt and my cheeks flame. My finger circles his dimples before pointing at his t-shirt. "This look is really working for you. Damn, you're fine as hell."

A brilliant smile lights up his face and my brain short-circuits.

"That's my favorite," I whisper in awe.

Ryker's forehead creases as he nods to tent. "Roasting in our little sauna?"

"Oh my God. No!" I snort. "Your laugh and smile are the best." My voice breaks at the emotion glittering in his soulful gaze. "That's my number one," I add softly.

His mouth drops to mine before he murmurs, "It's all because of you. Only for you."

I sag against him, pouring all my overflowing bliss into our brief kiss.

"You're wonderful and perfect and all for me," I say on a happy sigh.

"Damn straight, Sunshine. Before we get carried away, what should we do first?"

"I read about a designated area of the cliffs that's safe to jump from. That could be exciting."

Ryker nods and leads us to our pile of supplies. "Let's hike up the trail and check it out."

"And we can have dinner up there. Picnic style," I suggest while bouncing on my toes.

"Sounds delicious."

We set off up the path with matching grins lifting our lips, our clasped hands swinging between us. I'm carrying the basket with food and he's got the backpack with other essentials. We're totally winning at this camping stuff.

"Will your companies be all right while we're here? Or will you need to check in?"

Ryker chuckles and squeezes my fingers. "They're hardly mine. The big bosses hire me and hardly know who I am. They'll survive without the data dumps for a few days."

"I'm still not entirely sure what you do for them, other than keeping the bad hackers out."

"That's the gist. The rest is just boring details that would put you to sleep."

"Never. I wanna learn about your job. It's this entirely different world I have no clue about. I'm sure putting it all together is interesting."

"I dunno about that. Security software isn't glamorous but it's vital. If you're serious, I can show you more when we get back to a computer."

"If it's a part of you, I wanna know all about it."

"It's settled. I'll tell you everything." Ryker pulls me closer to wrap his arm around me. "What about Len's Looks? Let's talk about what you're planning for Denten."

I blow out a lungful of air. "It's intimidating, you know? I'm going to have the freedom to create whatever my heart desires. I'm not sure where to start and that's kind of overwhelming. There's too many wild ideas swirling around up here," I explain while tapping my temple.

"You're so talented, Sunshine. Once you get going, nothing will stop you."

Too bad I don't have your confidence. I'm terrified of failing, like my parents have always predicted." My stomach sinks at the thought of proving them right. That's not an option I'll consider.

Ryker pulls me to a stop. "Don't say stuff like that. You're going to be a huge success. I'll help with anything you need. Even just cheering you on in the workroom."

My eyes lock on his and something profound passes between us. I brush a soft kiss on his jaw. "You're truly something special. How did I get so lucky?"

"We were brought together for a reason," he explains before dusting my lips with his.

I lean into him and the basket bumps his leg, reminding us of our plans. Without another word, we climb the rest of the way before reaching the diving cliff.

After setting everything down, I stretch my arms out wide and spin in a slow circle. The entire lake is visible from up here and the glistening sight is breathtaking. The rocky trail continues around but is blocked by huge boulders. The waterfall must be close because the pounding echo practically vibrates through me. My eyes continue bouncing around the stunning space while Ryker spreads a blanket on the flat surface. I go to him and wrap my arms around his waist, holding tight as his heartbeat drums into my ear.

"This is incredible," I murmur softly.

Ryker hums, "It really is."

"You make me so happy."

He rests his chin on my head before saying, "You're the definition of that word."

"I'll love you forever, Ry."

I tilt my face up, seeking his warm embrace. Ryker swoops down immediately, not making me wait before pressing his lips to mine.

"I'll love you forever plus one, Sunshine," he hums into my mouth.

My tongue glides smoothly along his as we get lost in the kiss for a few beats, taking and giving from one another. My limbs turn to jelly when he pulls me closer while angling for a deeper connection. When we break away, our foreheads touch softly and the binds tying us together strengthen further. Current zaps between us as we get swept into oblivion, saying so much without uttering a syllable.

His nose brushes down mine and I shiver from the gentle caress.

"I can't believe this is real. My insecurities are still on a constant loop," he sighs against me. "What I feel for you is so powerful and all consuming. It's really difficult for me to comprehend you feeling the same way. I'm trying but it doesn't always add up," Ryker admits quietly.

"Well, I do feel the same. So much. And I'll keep telling you until you believe me. This is forever," I murmur quietly before placing a soft peck against his cheek.

His arms band tighter around my middle.

"Too bad I don't have a ring because this would be perfect timing," Ryker whispers into my neck. My breath falters as my heartbeat takes off at a full gallop. He pulls back while scanning my watery eyes. "Too soon? I know we've only been dating a very short while. I'm sure people would think we're rushing it but—"

"What they think or say doesn't matter," I blurt, picturing him down on one knee. The idea stirs up a hoard of the giddiest butterflies in my belly. "If we're happy and know it's right, that's what counts. We do what's right for us, always." I'm smiling so wide my cheeks hurt but when Ryker mirrors the expression, my mouth somehow stretches further.

"So, you'd say yes?" His pitch rises as if he can't believe my response.

I nod quickly before jumping up, my legs automatically finding a home around his waist. In the next moment Ryker's palms cradle my ass, as if that movement is instinctual too. "Wanna take the plunge with me?" I question against his jaw.

"Of course, but I don't have—"

My head gestures to the drop off in front of us. "Let's jump together. Seems fitting, right?"

Understanding dawns across his features and Ryker grins.

"Very," he murmurs along my lips and sets me down.

I kick off my sandals and shimmy out of my shorts before whipping off my tank. Ryker steps out of his shoes and his eyes widen while he scans my bikini-clad figure.

With a little swivel of my hips, I ask, "Do you like it?"

"You're too fucking hot," he groans. "Good thing we're about to cool off."

When Ryker ditches his shirt, my mouth goes dry at his muscular chest. I gulp loudly before fanning my face.

He reaches forward and laces our fingers together. His lips latch onto mine as he drags me closer. I let his mouth distract me and don't realize we're about to go over until the last second. My eyes dart down into the sparkling water and my feet shuffle nervously.

"Wait a minute. We're really high up. What if it's not deep enough? I might have miscalculated this part of the adventure," I reason weakly.

"Too late, you already suggested it." He chuckles before clutching my hand tighter. "This spot is meant for diving. Hold on, Sunshine. Ready?" Ryker asks while tugging me closer to the edge.

My muscles ache with tension as I stare into his blue depths, syphoning courage from him. In the next beat, my eyes squeeze shut as my nails dig into his skin. Everything within me clenches as I blindly nod. Then we're falling, soaring together, before crashing into the cold water. My system is shocked momentarily from the drop but quickly kickstarts triple time. We're completely submerged but Ryker's grip never falters as he kicks to the surface. I gasp after breaking through, sucking in air hungrily before blinking to clear my vision. When my gaze locks with his, we both start laughing.

"That was really fun," I pant while moving into him.

Ryker draws me closer with one arm before paddling us toward a shallow alcove.

"Your heart is pounding," he says while propping me against the cool stone wall but the chill doesn't faze me.

My concentration is securely fastened elsewhere.

I have a personal peepshow to his fantastic upper body, my sight overwhelmed by washboard abs and concrete pecs. It's like a switch is flipped and suddenly hot desire pumps through me. Ryker's ropey veins trail down his forearms and my fingers trace the curving tracks. My ankles cross against his ass before cinching the hold, which securely wedges him between my thighs. I'm deliciously pinned between his solid hardness and the unforgiving rock behind me.

"I'm excited," I purr while arching against him.

Ryker licks up my neck before asking, "For which part, Sunshine?"

Before surrendering to his worship, I manage to respond with a breathy murmur.

"Our entire future."

twenty-two

RYKER

I've been basking in the sunshine and forgot to watch for torrential downpours.

ALL TOO SOON OUR TIME at the lake has come to an end and it's time to head back.

We're going *home*.

I never had much reason to use that term before the brilliant ray of light currently sitting next to me in the truck strolled into my dark existence. Until we move to Denten in a few weeks, Lennon wants to spend our nights in the sunshine room. It'll be sad to leave that special spot but the sheer excitement of having our own space outweighs any melancholy. The studio loft in that sleepy little town is somewhere we'll share as a new chapter in our journey begins. Filling all the pages of our love story will be the greatest honor of my life.

We already have a great head start.

Lennon stares out the window, watching the campsite disappear into the distance.

"That was a magical trip," she sighs wistfully before facing me. "We'll have to visit again."

"All that alone time with you? Sign me up every day." I kiss her palm.

"Cuddling in that tiny tent," she replies softly.

"Watching the stars."

"Roasting marshmallows by the fire."

"Hiding out under the waterfall."

"Lounging on the raft."

"You in a string bikini with no one else around."

She chuckles before adding, "The jump was my favorite."

"And what happened right after." A groan rumbles from my chest.

"You're so bad." She swats my shoulder before I capture her hand again.

"Well, you're irresistible." My lips dust across her silky skin, sucking lighting on her wrist for a sweet taste.

Our playful banter continues the entire ride until we're pulling into the apartment parking lot. My head rests against the seat as I twist toward her.

"Where to next, Sunshine?"

Lennon bites her lip.

"A hot shower would be great. Maybe some packing. But for our firsts, did you see the billboard advertising that festival in Belleson next weekend? Where there's something fun for everyone?" She raises a brow in question. "I've never been to a carnival. Think of all the possibilities. The Ferris Wheel, cotton candy, fried food, tractor pull, those huge stuffed animals that aren't practical by any means," she rattles off the choices while I soak up her desire to spend time with me.

"Endless options," I say with a wink as a plan solidifies in my mind.

She blows me a kiss before hopping out. Warmth spreads through my chest before racing down my limbs. For once in my life, everything is perfect.

As I join her unloading the car, someone calls out.

"Lennon?"

She spins around and her eyes expand to saucer-size.

"Mom?" The question wobbles from her mouth. "Dad?" she sputters as her father steps out of the car. "What are you guys doing here?" Her fingers tremble in my grasp and I'm on instant alert as dread snakes up my torso.

"We came to convince you that moving further away is a mistake. It's clear just *showing up* was the right choice," her dad announces while glaring at me. "You," he points at me with a steady finger. "Get your filthy hands off my daughter this instant. I'm not sure what the hell's been going on but it's over now."

Lennon swallows loudly, the gulp dropping into my gut like a ton of lead.

"This i-is Ry-Ryker. H-he's my boyfr-friend," she stammers quietly. She stiffens her posture before adding, "I love him and he loves me."

"That's ludicrous," he snorts before crossing his arms in front of him, his weathered features stern and hard. "There's no way you expect me to believe you care for this man."

Her expression crumples from his tone and my fury barrels forward. Lennon tucks her chin before glancing at me.

"We're moving in together. Ryker is going to live with me." A small grin lifts the corner of her lips. She's so brave, my beautiful girl. Even in front of their misplaced ridicule, she shimmers bright.

"The hell you are," her father bellows but the gruff sound holds no weight. "What on God's green Earth makes you think we'll allow that?"

Lennon's eyes ignite into aqua flames as she pins him in her stare.

"You don't have to agree. I'm very much a consenting adult who's capable of making her own choices. Ryker and I are happy, and that's all that matters."

My chest swells with pride as her bold words sink into my pores, but her parents aren't packing up yet.

Her mother's audible gasp snags my concentration.

"Oh, my stars. This is getting out of hand! Lennon Elizabeth, you've been spending time with this . . . this beast of a man? He could hurt you!" she squawks and the shriek pierces my eardrums but I don't flinch. "He's the size of two men. What the hell is wrong with you? Can you not see the menace in his crazy looking eyes?" Her palms wave wildly toward me as she keeps spewing hate. "I knew you should have come home. There's no one here to keep you safe. Not even that worthless friend of yours. She's probably behind all this—"

"I keep her safe," I growl under my breath, full of fight and thunder. My interruption won't help their opinion of me but hopefully it'll tell them I'm fucking serious. And pissed the hell off.

"What did you say to my wife? How dare you talk to her that way," her father spits back at me. "Maybe we should call the police. I'm concerned you've brainwashed her into believing your bullshit."

Their harsh judgements bounce right off me, there's nothing they can say that will wound me. I've heard far worse and have no reason to listen. Lennon's mine and always will be. She told me we're forever and that's all I need. The lies they're weaving don't bother me and the verbal lashings cause no damage. My only concern is Lennon and keeping her safe.

I take a defiant step forward, covering her from their hateful stares as my shoulders set with steel.

"Go ahead. They'll appreciate knowing that you've come to where *we* live and are tossing out outlandish accusations. You're a bitter—"

"Ryker, please stop!" Lennon's sharp scold cuts me off. Her harsh tone is a slap across my face I wasn't expecting so her yanking grip around my flexed bicep goes unnoticed.

Ice dumps in my veins as she pulls me aside. I freeze next to her. My heart drops to the concrete through my feet, shattering into a million broken pieces around us. I can't run away or think of what to say, all that pounds into me is her resounding rejection. Lennon's lips are moving as she talks to me but all I hear is the whooshing of the past dragging me down.

My thoughts tunnel like they did that night in her apartment after I confessed to paying half the studio rent, but so much worse. What's happening now is my greatest fear warping into reality. My entire purpose and meaning has been keeping her safe from situations exactly like this but Lennon just shoved me away. She doesn't want my help. Or anything to do with me. Any hope or wish or pipedream shrivels up inside my stomach before burning away into fiery acid.

This feels like the end . . . of everything.

The only person I love is done with me and there's not a damn thing I can do about it except meltdown like the beast her parents believe me to be. Flames blast through my bones as I scan the area for an escape. I need to get the fuck out of here before my broken brain takes over and shit gets really psycho.

My only trigger left is pushed when Lennon turns away. Every painful memory comes flooding back. The volume on the degrading voices cranks up so all I hear is their venom.

Hulk.

Weirdo.

Loser.

Stupid.

Crazy Eyes.

It's like a low budget horror film flickering in front of me with each word as the hate blasts louder. The years of abuse and neglect from my parents. People shoving me away for being different. The constant bullying and harassment. The taunts and names that punctured my fragile soul. Being isolated and alone without hope of finding a way out. Everything Lennon has repaired shatters as a bolt slams into me. I've been stupid to believe she could actually care about me. This was all temporary and my logical brain screams at my gullible heart. I knew Lennon would get sick of me and now she has. I've been too pushy and clingy and needy and crazy.

Crazy. Crazy. Crazy.

I spiral further down with each passing moment but there's no more shits to give. All the light has been snuffed out of my spirit with a few direct hits.

Lennon keeps looking at me as her once tempting mouth forms words I can't make out. She reaches for my face but I dodge away from her touch, suddenly frightened of the impact her satin palm will have on me.

"Ry?" The nickname breaks through the fog but the dense clouds are too thick to see her sunshine.

"I understand." The barely-there rasp grates from my throat as I stare past her. "You don't need to explain it to me. You've made the choice. I'll go."

"What's happening, Ryker? I'm really sorry for being snappy. Did you hear me? They always test my patience but that's no excuse for my actions." Her teal eyes mist when I evade her fingers again. "Please, stop." Lennon's voice is weak but the use of the exact same words from before might as well be a roar. Everything else she says is drowned out.

My head jerks as I shift further away, mentally and physically.

"You'll always be my sunshine but this wasn't meant to last."

Tears stream down her rosy cheeks.

"Ryker, don't say things like that," she begs but the key to my wounded soul has been crushed to dust.

The need for my hood and the shield it offers from prying eyes consumes me. When I reach for the comforting cloak, all that's wrapped around my neck is empty air.

I never thought the one to leave would be me but it's clear that's what Lennon wants. All I truly want is to make her happy and I hold onto that thought as I sink into the shadows and her form blurs before me.

twenty-three
LENNON

"RYKER!" I CALL OUT BUT he keeps moving further away.

His retreat doesn't pause and sorrow hijacks my thoughts. Why the hell did I reprimand him for defending me? What the hell is wrong with me? Shame scorches my scalp as tears trickle from my lashes. A twitch attacks my hands, desperate to hold him, but he's refusing my touch. I lashed out for the first time in my life and it was directed toward the very last person who will never deserve it.

What effing twilight zone did I get dropped into?

The hollow glaze masking Ryker's ocean eyes is really freaking me out. The desolate indifference reminds me of how he looks at everyone else, but never me. At least until this moment. He's withdrawing from me and the loss pangs inside me.

"Ryker, please!" I try again, regardless of the hopeless feeling slithering up my spine.

Even in the summer heat, my teeth chatter from a gust of frosty wind that seems to swirl around my chilled form.

My sandals slap the pavement as I begin following him.

"Be serious, Lennon!" My mother's shrill cry stops me in my tracks. "We knew you'd find a boyfriend eventually but not like that behemoth. There's no way you actually expect us to approve of him."

I spin on my heel and stomp toward them. Anger like I've never experienced before streaks up my legs and races into my hollow gut, successfully burying me deeper in frigid numbness. The fury festers and spreads as my eyes narrow on their stern faces. Sharp and jagged icicles rise around me, hardening my backbone for what needs to happen. I've never stood up to my parents, all the unleashed hurt they've caused has been silently stewing inside. For years I've let them rule me but treating Ryker poorly is the last straw.

"You both need to leave. Now," I demand as my arm sweeps to the open road. Their stern features melt into expressions of concern but I'm too far gone. "How can you say such horrible things without even knowing him? Why? Your shallow accusations are disgusting," my voice is a rolling rumble.

Everything they've said is awful, but I'm the one to blame for turning this into an epic disaster. My throat burns with bile.

I need to fix this.

"Sweetie, listen to us. We know what's best, and that man is not it." My mother attempts to use a soothing tone but it falls flat. All I hear is static at this point, a broken record going round and round. "Let's go somewhere quiet to chat about your future. Maybe you'd like to come work at the firm after all? Give this designing business a rest for a bit? Clearly staying here has not been in your best interest," she says as she wrinkles her nose.

"I can't believe this." I swallow several times as my fingers spear into my hair, clutching hard at the roots. "Are you two for real? How about what I want? Do you care about me at all?"

I look between them and find nothing but scrutiny staring back. My face tilts skyward, asking for understanding from them. Hoping beyond hope that the people who raised me are better than this. Even in these moments of extreme distress, neither one reaches for me or offers comfort—not that it really matters since Ryker's touch is all I want.

How are these my parents?

I shake my head in dismay as they continue quietly staring at me.

"Never mind, don't bother answering any of that. I'm not going to keep standing here, pointlessly arguing, while the man I love is suffering." My voice cracks thinking of Ryker walking away. "He's my priority and always will be moving forward." My palm shoots out when my father tries piping in. "My time listening to you is over. If you'd like to apologize for the damage you've caused, maybe we'll try talking later." With that, I'm officially done—at least until they're ready to change.

As I stride off in the direction Ryker went, realization slams into me and my steps falter. Dammit, I should have known better. I caused all of this to happen. I'm such an idiot for snapping at him that way. All he was doing was trying to protect me and I shut him down. He had my back but I didn't have his. I've let him down in the worst way when we needed to stick together.

Shit, I'm the worst.

Fuck. How do I fix this?

I just promised to keep reassuring him of my devotion until he truly believed me but at the first test I failed. He's taking my harsh response as a forever betrayal against him, the rejection he's been predicting all along. I should never talk to him that way.

But it's more than me holding back impulsive reactions. I didn't want to rock the boat or tear up the resolved agreement we'd come to after our disagreement with the studio rent. All along I've been aware of his resistance. Ryker placed his fear of abandonment and insecurities under my nose but I didn't do a good enough job making him believe in my love. If we can't move past his fear of me leaving him, we'll never survive and that isn't an option.

I've been so wrapped up in planning fun adventures and the most vital first of all has been forgotten. My love for him needs to shine bright, like the sunshine he calls me. I need to ensure he feels cherished, wanted, adored . . . everything he's been starved of his entire life. My palm rests on my forehead as I take a shaky breath.

Why the hell am I still standing here?

It's my turn to pursue him for a change. It's a special way to reach Ryker that he'll understand. I snag a few necessary items from the truck before dashing across the lot. I pause halfway after realizing writing while walking isn't working. My hands get busy as my mind works double time to create unique phrases. Once my stack is complete, I continue tracing his path at a rapid rate. When I round the building, my fast pace stops short as my lungs seize.

Ryker's massive form is crumpled on the ground with his back against the brick wall. His handsome face hides behind his hands, as though his old black hood is shielding him from view yet he's out in clear sight. I settle beside him on the grassy lawn, giving him about a foot between us if he still wants space.

I clear my throat before whispering, "I'm so sorry, Ryker. I feel awful for what just happened and it's all my fault—"

"Go back to your family, Lennon." Ryker's voice is a despondent mumble.

"I'm looking at him," automatically drops from my lips and the truth clangs through me.

He scoffs.

"I mean it. You should leave. I'm no good for you."

"I'm not going anywhere. If you're here, so am I. If I say you're the best, the greatest of all, would you believe me?"

Ryker flinches slightly but remains hidden by his palms. "I'm bad fucking news, Lennon. Seems like you're finally starting to realize it too. I'm better off alone. That's what I'm used to, right?" The growl is fierce and sharp, a tone I haven't heard from him before.

I push forward, desperate for him to hear me beyond the layers of pain.

"I completely understand you walking away from me after my shitty behavior but that doesn't mean we're done. Not even a little bit. We're going to solve this once and for all. I'm never giving up on you."

"I won't drag you down anymore. I'm nothing, a total loser. Remember what they called me in school? I'm a freak, Lennon. A crazy eyed creep who will only wreck you. Anything else I say right now won't be good. There's been enough damage already. Go back with your parents where you're safe," he bites out with grit and venom. His self-deprecating jabs are like bullets to the chest, puncturing my skin and making me bleed.

My eyes sting as I ask, "Is that really what you want? What you actually think?"

"It doesn't matter what I say. You're going to leave regardless."

I sniff away the emotion clogging my throat. "That's not true, Ryker. Please don't push me away."

"Too fucking late." His wrist jiggles, spinning the bracelet I made him, as he asks, "Want this back?"

"That's something special for you," I answer quietly, trying to hide the hurt slicing into me.

"I don't deserve it," he rapidly retorts.

Ryker is beside me but seems miles away. This isn't my man. The savage misery has imprisoned him and I've gotta break him out.

"We love each other and belong together. Nothing you say will come between that—"

"Stop!" His roar ricochets through me but I don't follow his command.

Tears pool in my eyes as I choke out, "I'm so sorry, Ryker. I've ruined everything and failed you. Just the other day you asked me to always be there, walking with you, supporting you. At the first bump in the road, I've let you down and did this to us." I hiccup before grabbing the stack of notes by my hip.

"I choose you, Ryker." I read the first one and place it on his thigh. His leg twitches from the tickle of yellow paper.

"I want you, Ryker," I sob as the little square sticks to his knee. He scrubs down his face before peeking over at me, his ocean irises glistening with raw emotion.

In rapid succession, I set down message after message, my hoarse tone echoing the messy scrawls.

"You're all I've ever wished for."

"I'll never leave you."

"You are a good man, Ryker."

"Don't be afraid to fall with me."

"Together we're whole."

"I love you, Ry."

"Thank you for keeping me safe."

"I believe in us."

"You're my fantasy."

"Ry + Sunshine = 4EVA." That one earns me a dimple in his cheek.

The final one trembles in my fingers as I hand it to him.

"The sun wouldn't exist without the sky and moon and stars. Say you'll always be mine."

Ryker's brow rolls against his forearm as he turns to face me, a haze hindering my view his blazing blues. "You didn't let me protect you," he manages with a choppy exhale.

I curl my body around him, no longer caring if he'll push me away. Instead Ryker's arms cinch around me. We huddle close as I blab out a variety of gibberish along the lines of *I love you, this is forever, I'm so sorry, please forgive me, I'll do better, don't be afraid,* and *come back to me*. My grip clenches on his shoulders as he drags me tighter against his chest. Matching sniffles and murmured affections are exchanged in the small space as we cling together.

"Did you know I dream of your eyes?" I say after gaining a hint of composure. Ryker's wide orbs flicker to me before dodging away. "Your endless blues are like ocean waves I'm desperate to drown in. I could easily stare into your soulful depths and surrender to those restless tides," I share, recalling pieces of my favorite images. "Your irises are so much more than a simple color. There's a multitude of layers fighting for attention. What I see is swirling rapids covering a calm stream that's surrounded by the dark midnight sea. I saw those things even while you hid from me," I admit with a sigh. "Now I get the real deal each day."

"My Sunshine," he groans, clutching me with all his might, as if still afraid I'll take off at any moment.

I tuck my face deeper into the crook of his neck, the tears soaking my cheeks making them stick to his shirt. He smells like evergreen comfort and woodsy warmth, as if I'm near the crackling campfire again. Wrapped in his arms, the ice in my veins melts away and bubbling warmth flows through me. With a calming breath, I give him more. "We're made for each other, no matter what, and I've done a shitty job reassuring you. I didn't control everything that happened over there," I explain while blindly pointing over my shoulder, "and I take full responsibility for making it worse. I should have let you stand up for me, *for us*, but my past got in the way too. Those are my parents and I've always let them rule me so out of spineless habit, I tried stopping you from stepping in. Maybe as an attempt to shield you from their wrath or I was being a typical chicken shit, who knows. But no more.

"I love you and that's most important. They'll always be part of my genetic make-up but you're what truly brings me to life. Nothing comes between us," I grasp the fabric over his heart before nuzzling deeper into his embrace. "I can't survive without you, Ry. If I'm your sunshine then you're my sky. There can't be one without the other. *Please* never shut me out," I beg.

Ryker's palms scoop me by the rear before depositing me on his lap, immediately folding me into a tightly-knit hug. "I love you, Sunshine. I'd never last without your warmth but they'll never approve of me. Can you really live with that?"

"Yes," I answer without hesitation. "What I can't live with are the shadows lurking around us. We gotta put them to bed once and for all, yeah?" My jaw quivers with his shuddering exhale.

"Please tell me what to do," his broken plea cramps my stomach because for a moment, I picture his much younger self searching for support but everyone turns him away.

I stroke through his short scruff, my nails scratching against the coarse hair.

"There are times we might not agree on everything. Strange, right?" I huff out a short laugh and he presses a soft kiss to my temple. "I'm capable of being a brat once a month but my mood doesn't mean I don't love you. I'm here, one hundred percent in. You'll always have me and I'll try to prove it each day. But you've gotta have faith in me, Ry. You've gotta give me the benefit of the doubt sometimes."

"I always believe you," he says in a low timbre.

A soothing hum shimmies up my throat. "You've made it apparent how much you care for me but what about trusting that someone loves you? Wants to dote and spoil you for change? That's something you'll have to work on accepting but I'll do my best to relieve any stress. Giving yourself permission to be vulnerable after a life of hurt seems scary but we've gotta give more power to our connection by letting that guard down. I want us to be confident in our relationship, no matter what unexpected twists arise. There's no end for us, only new beginnings that will test our strength at times. Together we'll conquer all," I breathe along his throat and watch as my words cause goosebumps to rise.

Ryker shifts slightly, eliminating any space between us as our bodies melt into one clumped mass of energy. "I go where you go, always. No more doubt," he whispers into my hair.

"Only joy and celebration," I respond.

His lips twitch against my brow. "I've been waiting for you my entire life."

"You'll never be alone again."

"Thank God for that. I'm ready to start our life, for real this time." Ryker blows out a heavy breath.

I repeat his familiar phrase, the short statement packed with special meaning.

"Watch me follow."

twenty-four

RYKER

My heart and soul—everything I have worth a damn—remains with her. Always.

MY BODY JERKS AWAKE, IMMEDIATELY alert, yet my brain is groggy and disoriented as if I've been knocked out for a full eight hours.

Could that be possible?

Last night was emotionally and physically exhausting. I was convinced at one point that there'd be no tomorrow. What was there to live for if she wasn't around anyway?

When I stormed away from Lennon, my windpipe seemed to collapse as suffocation became a possibility. It leveled me. I struggled to breathe while black spots narrowed my vision until raw warmth blasted around the cold brick that had replaced my heart. When Lennon plopped next to me with no intention of leaving, my heart rejoiced and the poison slowly drained from my system.

For good this time.

We sat outside, snuggled together, while the light of day fizzled and the dark settled around us. When Lennon began shivering and her skin felt cool, we returned to the sunshine room. This space itself seemed to seal our reconciliation and solidified the declarations we'd exchanged.

"Good morning, sleepyhead," Lennon coos.

Her nails scratch along my scalp and delicious tingles take over my body. I moan and lean into her touch but realize she should be far closer. She's propped against the headboard, wearing way too many clothes, and a remedy for this entire situation becomes priority.

I reach around her back, gripping her slender shoulder, before tugging her down into the pile of fluffy bedding. She squeaks but doesn't complain, appearing pleased when I rest my head on her flat belly. Lennon's relaxing comforts continue, the massage threatening to pull me back under.

Lennon's happy turquoise gaze catches mine when I glance up.

"You make an excellent pillow," I tell her before nuzzling into her breasts. "But you should still be naked. I tore this shirt off you last night for a reason."

She clucks and raises a sculpted brow.

"We won't get anything done if you woke up to me totally nude. There's too much to do. I've been making plans while you slept. And first," she says as she rolls over to grab a plate by her hip, "you need to eat."

"You left without me?" The panic scratches my dry throat.

Lennon shakes her head before dusting my forehead with a

soft kiss.

"I cooked for you. Nothing too fancy. But the eggs are fluffy and the bacon is crispy."

My breath hitches and I blink rapidly to ease the sudden sting. "Nobody's done that for me before."

"Well, there's another first. With many more meals to come."

A satisfied rumble rolls from my chest. "Sunshine, you're spoiling me."

"It's about time I start pulling my weight around here," she says while her fingers softly stroke down my temple.

"You do plenty by just existing."

"Charmer," Lennon whispers.

I puff out my chest and say, "Damn straight."

She chuckles and a sweet smile pulls at her lips. Lennon lifts her hips, encouraging me to flip over, before setting the breakfast on my stomach.

"You enjoy this while I talk. I've decided we should leave for Denten today or tomorrow. We can make a few stops along the way, like the carnival this weekend. With all that's happened, I'm ready for a fresh start in our new home. Not that I'll ever forget this magical place you created here," she gestures toward the decorated walls. "But all these notes and memories can come with us. Whatcha say? I think this move will be really good for us."

"You're brilliant," I say between bites and cataloguing her glowing features. "Have I told you about your eyes changing color? Depending on your mood, they're either a bit greener or a tad bluer. There's also times when the two mix perfectly together, like a peaceful pairing."

Lennon's face creases as she asks, "What do you mean? My eyes are blueish-green, like aqua. They always have been."

I happily munch away for a moment, the seasoned eggs bursting with fresh flavor on my tongue, while enjoying the emotion flicker within her stare.

"It's something I've noticed about you over the last few weeks. When you're really excited, like right now, I see more blue peeking through. Last night, when you were angry and sad, green stole the show. It's been a way for me to tell how you're feeling. Pretty cool, huh?" I grin at her slack jaw and blushing cheeks.

"How do you . . . ? I mean . . . where did that, um . . ." Lennon bites her lip. "You're so freaking amazing, I can't even find the words. I'll never get used to how you see me, Ryker. Each day, you see deeper and it astonishes me," she whispers in awe.

Her thumb sweeps along my face, as if the soft pad is memorizing each pore. I kiss her finger when she reaches my mouth.

"It's all for you, Sunshine. Always. You stopped my suffering and I'll spend eternity showing how much that means to me."

"I love you so much, Ry." She swallows hard before blowing out a heavy exhale.

"And I love you," I echo while finishing my breakfast.

We lay silently for a beat before Lennon's phone vibrates on the dresser. She rolls her eyes and huffs after glance at the screen but doesn't comment further.

"Who is it? Lucy?"

"I wish. Hearing from her would be great. That," she points at the device as if it's possessed, "is my parents. *Again.* They've been messaging me all morning."

My breath falters as I imagine their words. "Aren't you . . . um, going to answer?"

"No. They don't deserve it."

"Please don't shut them out on my account."

Her head shakes wildly. "I'm ashamed of myself for how I acted around them. They always make me feel bad about myself. I don't need those bad vibes in my life," Lennon explains on a long sigh.

"What's worse than that is how they treated you. I can't forgive them for that. At least not so easily. It will be a long time before I'm ready to make amends."

"So, you're just going to keep ignoring them?"

Lennon shrugs. "Why not?"

My heartrate kicks up as a distorted vision of my parents flashes before me. I blink quickly to erase the image before clearing my throat.

"I wonder what growing up in a happy home is like," I say softly.

Her fingers smooth the wrinkle in my brow. "We'll have the happiest future to make up for it."

When her phone buzzes again, Lennon's nostrils flare as she blows out a stream of air.

"Maybe you should just answer."

"No. If anything, I'll write them a letter."

"Is that a thing between you guys?"

"I saw a therapist in my teens and she suggested it. I've written countless letters that they'll never see. It was a way to express myself without saying a word. Writing it all out gave me a voice when I didn't have one," Lennon mumbles.

After a beat, she keeps going. "In this case, I'd actually send it. That way I'm not ignoring them and they'll know how I feel."

"I should do that too."

Lennon kisses my forehead before asking, "To your mom and dad?"

My teeth grind at the mention of them but a calming inhale forces the anger away.

"Yes. I never want to think of them again but maybe releasing the hurt they caused will allow me to let them go. For good. What's the worst that could happen, right?" I shoot her a small smirk but inside my stomach bubbles with fear.

What if pouring out the painful history on paper releases festering injuries that refuse to close? What if they linger and ruin my life again?

I twist a lock of Lennon's long dark hair before announcing, "I'll do it."

"We can write together. Another first without even planning it. How 'bout that, huh?" Her silky tone slinks around me. "We'll beat them all, Ry."

"Everything is possible because of you, Sunshine."

"You give me far too much credit."

"Clearly, I haven't done a good enough job explaining how terrible my life was without you," I say while she purses her lips. "Should I start from the beginning?"

Lennon shakes her head. "No, no. We're good. I'll accept your praise if you take all mine. Deal?"

"Deal."

"You're very agreeable today," she points out.

I scoff in mock offense.

"Why wouldn't I be? I've got you in bed, promising to be in my life forever. Things aren't too shabby for me. I'd say they'll be even better quite soon," I suggest without giving her more info.

She might have planned an impromptu road trip but I've got a secret agenda item to tack on. If Lennon has any idea I'm hiding something, she doesn't reveal it.

"Should we get going then?"

"Absolutely," I reply as anticipation attacks my system.

Almost everything was packed and ready to go before camping except for the words that litter this entire room. We spend the morning removing the messages one by one until Lennon has held and read each one. I assure her that a spot in our new loft will be dedicated to the little yellow squares. A dopey smile stretches my lips when I recall her notes to me. Those will definitely have a special place too. I glance over at Lennon, hair piled on top of her head and a flowy short dress covering her succulent curves, and I count my fucking blessings twice.

This girl gets me.

Soon enough we've triple checked for any forgotten items, stuffed the truck to the max, and are ready for whatever tonight brings us.

I'm hoping for a yes.

twenty-five

LENNON

Every single one of my firsts belongs to you. I want you to have them all.

"RY, I'M FALLING! SLOW DOWN!" Another obnoxious squeal peals from my lips as I flop against his back.

My legs tighten around his waist while I cling to his chest as Ryker continues bounding gleefully through the rowdy fairgrounds. His head turns to me as he laughs loudly.

"Your first piggyback ride is meant to be bumpy and ridiculous. I'd never let you go," he reassures me while squeezing my bare thighs.

We've only been here for an hour but I'm already having the best time. Ryker scarfed down an order of cheese curds while I stuffed my face with cotton candy. We went round and round on the Ferris Wheel, exchanging plenty of heated kisses and teasing touches. The ride ended with both of us extra hot and bothered but the sexual frustration morphed after a few obviously rigged carnival games.

Ryker hops to a stop near the carousel and swings me around to his front. The move is smooth and polished, as if he's done it a hundred times. Somethings work easily the first try, like us, figuring it out as we go.

"I always knew it would be like this," I murmur into his ear.

"What would be, Sunshine?"

I sigh softly, the bliss rushing out of me and into him.

"Being here, in love with you. Having a bright future, because of you. Starting a happy life together and having the freedom to choose whatever we want. The list is full of endless possibilities. Do you see it?" I ask after pulling away to stare into his relaxed blue orbs.

"I've always seen it, Sunshine," he mumbles while rubbing our noses together. "Since the very beginning and for the rest of our lives."

He pushes my back against the chain-link fence near the carousel before dropping his lips to mine, my mouth opens immediately so his tongue can stroke inside. The rainbow of fluorescent bulbs casts an iridescent glow and this moment is magical. My fingers race up his neck to drag against his buzzed hair, the friction from my nails has him moaning into me. I answer by sucking his lip between my teeth, nipping and nibbling the plump flesh. Ryker shoves me harder into the metal behind me just as someone makes a gagging noise.

"Getting a fucking room. We don't wanna watch that nasty shit," some stranger shouts at us.

Ryker's posture stiffens in my arms at the taunting and the

lid to my newly discovered temper loosens, ready to lash out at the interruption. These idiots should get an earful from me but I take a deep breath to avoid a fight.

"It's okay, Ry. They're just a bunch of assholes," I reassure him.

He dusts my lips in a scorching kiss before breaking away again.

"I could care less about those losers or what they think. Let them fucking gawk. I've got the most gorgeous girl with me, of course they're jealous." He smirks against my answering grin, the expressions blending into a radiant display of affection as our lips brush. "What bothers me is them wanting us to hide how we feel. We've been locked away far too long already, there's no going back. I'm ready to show off to anyone willing to look," he proclaims in a volume meant to be heard.

As more barbs and jeers are tossed at us, he's able to throw the ridicule away like the worthless words they are. This guy slays me a little more each day. His confidence finally shines through and the sight is truly astounding. Ryker is inspiration personified, a warrior surviving a lifetime of misery, and I'm the one here to witness it.

"Sunshine? Are you alright? Want me to shut those jerks up?" He asks quietly, the concern heavy in his deep voice.

I shake my head and gulp in some fresh air.

"I love you so much, Ry. That's all."

"Well, good thing I love you more," his voice is clear and sure.

Before I can argue, our mouths fuse again. Maybe to prove a point but also because we can't stop the pull. Lips glide and tongues tangle, never getting enough of the erupting sparks our connection offers.

Ryker jerks away and pants, "Let's go into the Fun House."

"Now? But—"

"Trust me, I'm all for exposing our love but certain things are meant just for us."

Excited tingles spread out from my lower belly. If he's cool with acting on our building lust, I guess it's another first to cross off the list.

Ryker laces our fingers before striding off in the direction of the neon painted building offering an array of mazes, mirrors, and wacky wonder. My clammy palm sticks to his but I don't mind the heat. My mind is caught up on the sensual slide I hope we'll feeling very soon.

I see Ryker hand the attendant money before murmuring, "Keep everyone else out for at least twenty minutes."

The guy's eyes widen as he peeks at the cash, clearly impressed with the amount. "You got it, buddy. Have fun!" He exclaims behind us as we rush into a dark tunnel.

We duck under some low ceilings before weaving through a twisted hallway, chuckling and giggling the entire way. I'm all turned around and couldn't find the exit if forced but apparently that's okay for a bit. We stumble into a room where mirrors cover every surface. The reflections stop me in my tracks. All around me, every direction I turn, is us. Red faced, mussed hair, matching grins plastered on our faces, and totally in love. The vision injects me with a direct hit of sentimental goo and suddenly I want some mush with the steamy stuff.

"Why do you love me?" I ask Ryker while turning toward him, no longer staring at our reflection but at the man in front of me.

He hums softly as his ocean waves crash into me.

"I think a better question is why not?"

I give him a sassy eyebrow, reading his obvious excitement

but demanding sweet seduction first.

Ryker chuckles before drawing me into his arms.

"Well, for starters you're super-hot," he says and I elbow his side. After an exaggerated *oof*, he pecks my forehead and continues. "You're my sunshine, a beam of guiding light in all the shadows. The air that keeps me living, the blood that allows my heart to beat, everything good that's ever been. You give me purpose where there wasn't any. Because of you, there's happiness. You're the only one who sees me . . ." His voice trails off.

We're quiet for a few beats and restlessness begins prodding at my spine.

"Don't you wanna ask me why I love you?" I question softly after tucking my chin.

He takes a step back before clasping my left hand in both of his. "There's actually something else I want to ask you, Sunshine." Ryker takes a shuddering breath and my mind whirls with possibilities. "I know there's a lot to be done that won't happen overnight. I'm a work in progress, but I'm yours. I'm your weirdo and you're my goofball, we make sense together. Maybe we're not normal or typical by average standards, definitely not perfect, but I'd rather be different with you regardless. Fuck fitting in and screw everyone against us. We'll fight on the same side, all day and night. I'll be your team, just us two against the world," he whispers before wiping the tears from my cheeks. I'm crying uncontrollably but can still see him clearly, the words from his mouth ring loudly in my ears. "Thank you for loving me, Lennon," he utters quietly before kissing my wrist.

Ryker drops to one knee and a gasp escapes me without warning but the shocked sound is expected. Shiny beams cast off the reflective surfaces, attempting to draw my gaze away but

I'm locked on his glittering eyes. His grandest gesture of love is being displayed all around us by this house of mirrors, but all I see is Ryker in front of me.

"We don't have to get married tomorrow or the next day but sometime. For now, just wear my ring and promise to love me always. Will you trade your name for mine and marry me, Sunshine?" Ryker asks with tears streaking down his face. He opens a small velvet box and the contents make me dizzy.

"Ryker! Is that a—"

"Sun? Yes," he cuts in smoothly. "I had it custom made, just for you. It's as unique and different as we are. Will you be my sunshine forever?"

I'm already nodding but shout *yes* several times for good measure. Ryker slips the ring over my knuckle, the blazing yellow diamond winking at me as it nestles on top of my finger. The brilliant center rock is surrounded by swirling and swooping rows encrusted with smaller clear stones, mimicking the sun with flames surrounding it. The countless gems sparkle in the mirrors, twinkling like real stars, but we're not paying attention.

My eyes bounce between my fiancé and the symbol of our future while his never waver from me. Ryker's hands cup my jaw before tilting my face to him. His thumbs swipe under my eyes before he melts my soul a bit more.

"So much blue looking back at me," he informs before blessing me with a searing kiss, locking us together in more ways than one.

epilogue
RYKER

I've lived a life of mayhem and destruction, a chaotic tornado sent to ruin. Everyone knew to steer clear, and give me plenty of space to pass in a flurry, except Lennon. Beyond reason and control, she approached the storm with a smile on her face.

~ Four Months Later ~

MY FINGERS PAUSE ON THE keyboard as the smell of fresh cookies wafts into the studio. I eagerly inhale the sugary scent, my lids sliding shut as the chocolate goodness soaks into me.

Darla, the owner of Betcha Buns, must be baking up a storm for the annual Frozen Days celebration. I've developed quite the sweet tooth thanks to her decadent desserts. Probably doesn't hurt that the bakery is next door.

I glance out the window and watch the bustling activity buzzing along Main Street. It seems like everyone in town is flooding the sidewalks for the upcoming holiday season. I smile as the vibrant joy spreads through the air.

Denten was a good choice for us.

An upbeat tune from the radio pulls my focus from the people milling by. My eyes land on my future wife as she shimmies her hips while securing fabric to the dress form. Lennon's glossy brown hair whips around with her movements and I'm hypnotized by the flowing waves.

She's so beautiful.

It's a shame to interrupt her dancing but she'll be shaking her butt again in no time.

"Sunny?"

Her aqua orbs lift to me as she mumbles, "Hmmm?"

"You're adorable," I chuckle as she struggles to speak around a mouthful of pins.

Lennon winks while pulling them from her lips. "What's up, Ry?"

"There's a ton of people out there," I say while gesturing outside. "Still ready to open tomorrow?"

Her features light up with a huge grin. "It's going to be perfect. This is the ideal time of year to start selling directly from the shop. Best idea yet."

"We make a great team."

"That we do, Ry."

The low hum from the sewing machine kicks in as Lennon sits at her desk. The yellow notes I gave her this morning are stuck on top of her work station, right where she can read them while finishing final touches.

I'm so proud of you, Sunny.
You're so brilliant and
talented and tomorrow the
town will finally get to
see what I've known all along.
I love you. I love you.
I love you.

A happy sigh escapes me while recalling the stunning joy covering her features. Each time I give her a yellow square, it seems like the first time. She loves those little pieces of paper and her reaction always chokes me up.

I clear the emotion from my throat. "Pretty soon everyone in Denten will be wearing Len's Looks. This town is practically begging for more clothing store options. The grand opening will be intense," I murmur with nervous energy skittering under my skin.

This is a huge opportunity for Lennon, *for us*, but a herd of people trampling into our sanctuary freaks me out.

As if hearing my internal struggle, she laughs lightly, "But not too crazy. We'll just play it by ear. If by some wild chance a crowd forms, we can call Darla for backup."

The tension bubbling within me evaporates with a chuckle. "She'd love that. Pretty sure she'll be over here the entire day regardless."

"Speaking of, have you talked to her about the cake samples?"

"Not yet. I've been waiting until her coconut frosting arrived. You know that's my favorite flavor," my voice rasps.

Lennon's cheeks flush and she giggles softly. "You're so romantic."

"Damn straight. Need an extra hand over there?"

She holds up her palm. "I've gotta finish these two dresses. You need to talk to Darla. Once she catches wind of our approximate wedding date, she'll want to start planning."

"No doubt about that," I sigh and picture Darla's glee. That woman has become like a mother to me and will surely go way over the top with this project. The upcoming months flicker through my mind and excitement unfurls in my gut. Lennon is going to look stunning in all white.

"There hasn't been much typing going on over there, Mister Doxson." Lennon's melodic tone breaks me from my thoughts.

"Too busy thinking of you, Soon-To-Be Missus Doxson." I shoot her a smirk.

Her blue-green eyes peek up at me from behind the sewing machine, the project laid out in front of her temporarily forgotten. A pink hue paints her face and my chest puffs wide knowing I've made her blush twice already.

She bites her lip before muttering, "Such a sweet talker."

"You know it, Sunshine. Getting hungry? Wanna visit Darla with me?" I suggest while rubbing my stomach, picturing the yummy goodness she'll have waiting next door.

Her head bobbles back and forth. "Let me finish this row of stitches quick. Maybe we can wander down to Sally's for some hot coco after?"

"Extra marshmallows?"

"Obviously," she scoffs.

"That's the good stuff."

Lennon snickers while adjusting her grip on the colorful material. "I'll show you some great stuff later."

"Tease," I call out and she winks wickedly before blowing me a kiss.

This is our new routine, working together at Len's Looks

during the day and snuggling upstairs all night.

What could be better?

Maybe sharing a last name but I'm not pushing the subject. We aren't in a huge hurry to get married—I'm more than happy to have her wear my ring. I've got something extra special in the works for after we're husband and wife though.

Her sunshine diamond glitters from the light pouring through the front windows as she feeds the machine more detailed fabric. I believe this piece includes lyrics from her favorite song written out in binary code. The seams are decorated with lines of the computer language many in the fashion world don't understand. To them, the pattern of numbers and the occasional letter looks like nonsense. A jumble of undefined meaning, scrambled beyond reason, but it looks cool as hell.

That's what sets apart the *Seeking Sunshine* collection, the designs are uniquely ours. We've collaborated to build a brand that incorporates both of us.

The clothes are being sent out into the world but only we know the love story written into the designs. My eyes sweep the room, checking out the array of merchandise, as pride swells within my chest.

The shirt draped over a dress form includes a few lines from my proposal that's been encrypted as a string of green code. The number sequence loops around the bottom half of the blue material is an elegant swirl. The rack of dresses in the corner include words describing several firsts we've experienced. The code loops around the neckline, traces down the zipper, and ends around the hem. There's a pile of yellow tank tops folded on the table that have messages from her favorite sticky notes. Every piece is different, exactly how she wanted them.

All of our sales come from online but that's about to change when we open the doors to local customers. I'm confident news will spread of the diverse styles Lennon's magical fingers create. The hidden messages we've included gives the collection an added edge that people will want to wear.

So far, business is booming and all her dreams are really coming true.

I silently watch Lennon work, pouring so much soul into each fluid movement. I asked her once if she was happy and held my breath waiting for her response. Now, I always see the joy clearly in the blue of her aqua eyes and feel the bliss with each cherished touch.

This is what love is.

Separately we were two broken halves, misunderstood and hopelessly waiting for someone to look beyond the jagged edges. Together we've defined a new normal—a beautiful life that's vibrant and different and ours.

"Whatcha looking at, Ry?" Lennon questions with a knowing smile lifting her perfect lips.

"You. Always you, Sunshine."

acknowledgements

WOW. I'M STILL A TAD shocked Watch Me Follow is done and published. This story was a tough one for me, in so many ways, and I honestly couldn't have survived without my amazing crew of support. I'm extremely blessed and honored to have so many fantastic people in my corner rooting me on.

My husband deserves some kind of fancy award for taking on double the work while I completed this book. He's honestly the greatest life partner I could ask for and am beyond lucky to have him by my side. Without him, being an author would remain a pipe dream, so I owe my guy everything.

A huge thanks to my family for their endless outpouring of love and encouragement.

What can I say about Ace Gray? She's taught me countless lesson that at times were very tough but extremely meaningful. My writing is better and my stories are stronger because of her. She's brilliant and talented and I'm thankful she's my friend.

I owe Talia, from Talia's Book Covers, a ton for her hard work and dedication to my books. She's always there when I need her, without a second of hesitation. I've found the meaning of true teamwork with this lovely lady. Her designs are gorgeous and her talent is limitless.

I'm so very glad to Melissa in my life. Her bright personality and constant help keep me going. When I first started writing Watch Me Follow, she was there to truly see what the story meant to me.

Cindy is fantastic and wonderful and an amazing friend. She's always there with warm advice and kind comfort. Thank you for everything!

Thank you SO much Ella, Annie, Devney, Kate, Victoria, Leigh, Penelope, Suzie, Sunniva, Tia, Monica, Lauren, Kahlen, Brittany, and many more for being so helpful with everything and anything. You're a spectacular group of ladies that I'm very lucky to consider friends. The author community is extremely supportive and I owe you all so much for continuing to encourage me.

To my reader group—Harloe's Hotties is my happy place and I enjoy our little slice on social media so much. Thank you all for the love and happiness you bring!

THANK YOU to my brand new Harloe's Review Crew. I'm eternally grateful for everything you guys do for me on a daily basis. All the shares, likes, comments, tags, messages, and support mean SO very much. An extra-large thanks to Julie, Megan, Jacqueline, Nancy, and Shauna for everything, all the time.

I'm very fortunate to be part of the #squadpod. Nicole, Jane, Jessica, JL, Kim, Liv, Paige, Brooke, Meg, Ava, and CL—you guys are awesome and I'm so glad we're a tribe!

A big shout out to the Do Not Disturb Club / DND Authors. All of your guidance, support, ideas, encouragement, and teamwork means a lot to me.

A special note to my fellow besties—Margie, Bobbie, and Jen—we've been together a lot of years and are still going strong!

Crystal and Maggie were the first bloggers to review Redefining Us. They've been with me from the start and have been promoting me ever since.

A huge thank you to my beta and proofreaders—Cindy,

Melissa, Angela, Bobbie, Shauna, Cyndy, and Nancy.

My formatting was done by Christine with Type A Formatting and she is fantastic to work with. She's the reason the interiors of my books look so pretty!

I'm extremely grateful to the bloggers that have helped promote my releases and spread the word to their followers. It's impossible to reach new readers without their endless dedication to this fantastic book community. They keep a big smile on my face. I deeply appreciate each and every single post, mention, and share. THANK YOU!

I'm beyond honored to have so many wonderful readers enjoy my work. An author needs her book junkies and I'm very grateful for each one of you. Thank you for the motivational messages, tags on posts to spread the word, and all the interaction we have. Most importantly, thanks for loving romance!

Last but definitely not least, thank you to those that have taken time to read and review my books. Words cannot properly express how much that means to me. Thank you, thank you, thank you!

about The author

HARLOE WAS BORN AND RAISED in Minnesota. She is married to an amazing man and they have an adorable son. These boys are what make life worth living. Harloe has a day job that she loves and is also passionate about horses, blogging, country living, and having fun.

Harloe has been in love with romance since she was a little girl reading fairytales. The dream is to find the perfect person that completes your life, right? Novels have a way of bringing fantasy to reality and she's always up for an unforgettable adventure.

Stalk Harloe on her blog (insert link to word blog: www.harloe-rae.blog) or send her a message at *harloe.rae@gmail.com*

also by Harloe

Redefining Us
Forget You Not

Continue on to read a bonus epilogue.

~ Another four months later ~

"READY?" I ASK WHILE STILL covering Lennon's eyes.

Her excitement is clear when she says, "You're finally going to show me?"

"Sunny, this is your wedding present and honeymoon all wrapped in one fancy bow. It took a bit of planning."

"Yeah, and a long ass flight. At least we got to cuddle in those cushy chairs."

"You're really complaining about first class, Mrs. Doxson?"

A wide smile stretches her glossy lips. "I'll never get sick of being called that."

"Good, because that's forever. And so is this," I say before lifting my hands and revealing her surprise.

Even from my spot behind her, I see the shock flicker through Lennon's features as she takes in our surroundings. She's given me everything so I'm returning the favor.

"Paradise," she sighs.

If possible, the word holds more awe than it did the first time she said it all those months ago.

Mission accomplished.

This is another first. A huge one.

Lennon has *strongly* requested—several times—that I don't spend frivolous amounts of money on her. I found a big loophole because Sunshine never said anything about buying stuff for us. This place is definitely ours.

"What do you think, Sunshine?"

She sniffs and glances at me quickly before her eyes dart back to the house.

"It's absolutely perfect."

Hidden in a private cape, out of sight and mind from anything close, is our little piece of tropical perfection. Every detail she once described is stretched out before us. Our exotic island home has been replicated from her whimsical musings and built in the ideal spot off the beach. The expansive fortress is far enough away so the ocean tides won't cause an issue but near enough that we'll hit warm sand within a few yards from the backdoor.

The exterior is painted a bright shade of yellow, the exact hue of Lennon's favorite notes. The color pops out against the vibrant green foliage that envelopes the structure. Expansive windows make up the entire ocean-view wall but it's difficult to tell at the moment. The glass is currently covered with countless little squares of paper, each with a special message, just as I requested.

Even from this distance, I can see the papers fluttering in the breeze.

The caretakers deserve a huge raise.

The rest of Lennon's vision fit together naturally, which is why I chose this location. The clear-blue sea laps gently against the white shore. There's not a single cloud in the sky, just miles and miles of light blue. The sun reflects off the water just right so the surface looks like a mirror. With a deep inhale, the salty wind settles into my lungs.

I wrap Lennon in my arms as we absorb the beauty around us. My body takes notice of her ass nestled against me and I pull her even closer. My fingers twine with hers, matching symbols of our love blend and brush together. The wedding bands represent our marriage, the promises we'll always keep. The tattoos circling our right ring fingers symbolize forever, the permanent ink bonding our souls in a seal of eternity. It was Lennon's idea—a bold sunshine breaking apart the storm clouds—because together, everything makes sense. One is nothing without the other and that's how she describes us. We belong with each other—always.

"From this day forward, for the rest of my life, I'll do everything to make you happy," I murmur softly into her ear.

Lennon hums, "I love our vows. Keep going, Mr. Doxson."

"We'll walk this life together, through shadowed darkness or blinding light . . ." I continue reciting the rest between soft kisses to her neck.

She nuzzles into my bearded cheek. "I can't believe this is our life. And it's all because of you."

"Because of us," I amend.

"I love you, Ry."

"And I love you, Sunshine." I swallow the lump in my throat

before telling her, "I'd do it all over again."

Lennon tips her head up to look at me. "What?"

"Dealing with my parents, the bullies, the anxiety, the loneliness . . . all the pain. I'd walk through that hell with a smile on my face because you'd be waiting at the end. Ready to offer comfort and unconditional love. I'd spend eighteen years in the dark for a lifetime of light."

"It was all worth it," she adds while lifting trembling fingers to my cheek.

We simultaneously exhale, mostly in happiness, maybe with a bit of relief too.

"Should we take a tour?" I ask after a few beats of shared silence.

She nods eagerly and lets me guide her along the sandy path. As more of the house comes into view, Lennon gasps. "Is that an—"

"Outdoor shower?" I finish for her. "It sure is. With heated tiles."

"Oh, my. Can we start there?"

"Absolutely," I say before dropping a searing kiss to her sweet lips. When I pull back, her aqua eyes are dazed and sparkling like precious stones.

An easy smirk curves my mouth. "Welcome to happily ever after, Sunshine."

Made in United States
Orlando, FL
18 December 2021